Hoofbeats on the Wind

Pamela Kavanagh

Hoofbeats on the Wind

Copyright © 2004 by Pamela Kavanagh
Original title: Hoofbeats on the wind
Cover and inside illustrations: Milja Holländer
Cover layout: Stabenfeldt Inc.
Published by Pony, Stabenfeldt Inc.
Edited by Kathryn Cole
Printed in Germany

ISBN: 82-591-1158-6

Prologue

They came drumming over the bleak stretches of the moor at a gleeful canter, a whole herd of wild ponies, tough, shaggy-coated, free.

As I gazed at them in open wonder, a little flame of joy sparked and flared within me. I could feel it spreading, filling me with warmth, chasing away the shadows. The ponies came on in a rush, snorting and tossing their heads, their eyes glinting white as they raced against the wind. I caught the hot, sweet, grassy smell of them and felt the ground tremble as they swept past with defiant kicks of their heels. Some of the mares had foals at their sides, leggy babies with little tufts of tails and innocent eyes. Their tiny hooves twinkled gamely over the sheep-nibbled turf as they strove to keep up with the rest. All at once I wanted to catch one of those ponies, to clamber up onto its rough broad back and gallop on forever.

I forgot my unfamiliarity with the countryside. I forgot Hob Tor, the dark peak that rose so eerily in the distance. I even forgot about the stark stone cottage on the empty fringes of moorland that Mom and I now called home.

A pony. We had a stable and a field – well, of sorts. Why not get a pony to live in it?

Chapter One

"Shelley? The men have finished now. Wouldn't mind some help down here, please."

Mom's voice echoed up the uncarpeted stair to where I was half-heartedly stacking books from a box onto my bedroom shelf. At the front gate, the tailgate of the moving van went up with a rush and a slam. The vehicle choked into life and went rumbling off down the desolate country road, bound for the highway and the long haul back to the seaport we had left behind in the misty dawn.

Home. We had only just arrived and already I was missing our old life.

"Shelley?"

"Coming, Mom."

Hastily I shoveled the final books onto the shelf, and picking a way through the half-emptied cardboard boxes and wardrobe containers, I shut the door on the chaos of my new bedroom under the eaves and went clattering down the stairs to even worse chaos in the kitchen.

Indignant yowls met me from the cat carrier on the table where Ming, our Siamese, was making a noisy protest of her own.

"Hi, Ming," I said with quick sympathy. "Want to come out?"

"Better not. She might escape and we don't want to lose her after all the effort to get her here." Mom glanced up from rummaging in a carton. Her long braided brown hair was coming adrift from the gauzy scarf it was threaded with and there was a smudge of dust on her nose. Her pretty face was harassed. "Can't find the coffee anywhere, Shelley, and I'm absolutely gasping for a cup."

"Maybe you put it with the groceries," I said, doubtful, since Mom was not the most organized of persons. Her idea of packing was to bundle everything blithely together and trust it would get sorted out at the other end.

"Don't think so... hey, got it!" With a small yelp of triumph Mom withdrew the missing item from a bundle of towels and brandished it high. "Coffee coming up!"

Much later, exhausted yet unable to sleep, I lay in my bed, staring out through the uncurtained window and listening to the deep country quiet that enveloped us as darkness descended. Conditioned as I was to the nighttime throb of a big city, I found that silence unnerving. Every bone in my body ached. Mom must have had us move the piano ten times at least, before finding a spot in the living room that suited her. Where things went had never been a problem in our old apartment.

A sliver of new moon sailed over the bare black reaches of the moor. Watching it, my mind backtracked to Mom, telling me she had gotten the teaching contract she'd applied for. It was a real credit to her. This foreign exchange music program was well known and highly regarded. She deserved the position and the chance to

7

teach talented students. I was proud of her but my heart had stopped momentarily.

"It will mean a big move, Shelley. England's a long way from here."

It wasn't the time to change my mind. We both needed a new start, especially Mom. She'd been through so much and I knew she wanted to return to England where she had been born. I'd get used to it, and even though I'd miss my friends, I was excited about the prospect of a whole new start in a brand-new place. Now that we were here, I'd pushed back my inner doubts more than once, In for a penny, in for a pound, as Mom often said.

Scrolling through real estate websites, we had stopped at a picture of a stone cottage with a big garden.
"What about this?" Mom asked. "Price is right. It's had a lot done to it as well – a big plus. And just look at those views. Dad would have approved."

True. Dad would have immediately taken up his camera and gone striding off into those open tracts of moorland in search of wildlife to photograph, moving with that eager, all-powerful energy he'd had before illness had sapped it. Tears had gathered, blurring Mom's anxious face. It had been months, but I still missed Dad as much as ever.

"Come on, sweetheart." Mom had put her comforting arms around me. "It'll be fine. Promise. You are excited about our decision, aren't you?"

Of course I was. I simply couldn't stop myself. When Dad's illness had been diagnosed as terminal, he had encouraged Mom to enroll for teacher training in the subject in which she was already well qualified – music.

Teaching's got a lot going for it. You'll both get the

same holidays for a start. Got to keep a roof over your heads, Lissa.

Stoically Mom had juggled studying with looking after Dad and earned her diploma. The vacancy in the music department of the English school renowned for turning out budding instrumentalists was made for her. Of course I was excited and I said so.

"There, then. We'll be fine," Mom said again.

Inwardly I was less sure, but willing to trade America for England, city life for country life.

Arrangements had gone ahead with lightning speed. We'd packed up and shipped our things, said goodbye to friends, and set out on our great adventure. It was now the summer holidays and here we were. Mom was going to the school in the morning to prepare for the term ahead, while I would be doing… what?

At least the house had turned out better than we expected. Two centuries old and low roofed to take the buffeting of the upland wind, with small windows set deeply into the gray stone walls, Rock Cottage sat staunchly on the very edge of the moor. We had more space here than at home, having three bedrooms instead of two and the lovely big living room downstairs. Mom had made curtains of glowing silk that would billow vibrantly once we got around to hanging them. Our fringed and patterned rugs already looked great on the polished wooden floors, and Mom's collection of lusterware and Dad's award-winning photographic studies made the place more like ours.

Mom had allotted me the best bedroom that looked out over the moor and a hill whose jutting peak seemed to pierce the sky.

Now it looked freaky, that hill. Silvered in pale moon-light, it seemed a place of secrets, and as I stared a small shiver of foreboding crept over my skin. Swallowing, I tossed over in the bed, thumping my pillow and burrow-ing down under the duvet in a renewed attempt to sleep. But still my mind played on.

Prior to moving, Mom had asked me to dismantle the home computer. I set about it methodically, color-coding the various plugs and sockets so that setting it up again would be straightforward. Before unplugging, some im-pulse made me first check for E-mails. Often Granny and Granddad Rees in Richmond sent one for fun.

This was from Bryce. Bryce Minton was my godfa-ther and, being a close friend of my parents, proved an absolute rock when Dad died. He's tall and good-look-ing in a craggy sort of way, and he always had a special smile for Mom, as if he liked her very much. The mes-sage was for her, one she had typically forgotten to put out of sight in her mailbox.

Lissa. Don't miss out on this job just because of cir-cumstances.

At that moment Mom had called me. I'd shut down the machine and that was that. Odd thing, during the week that followed Mom seemed a bit distracted, as if she were having second thoughts about the move. It came to nothing, and swept along on the tide of packing and goodbye parties, the incident had slipped my mind until now.

Yawning widely, I wondered what the message was about. What circumstances? It was a puzzle.

On that note I fell asleep, only to dream that Ming had escaped her traveling box and was padding purposefully back to her old stamping ground – how she managed to cross the Atlantic I don't know, but she made it back to the familiarity of the big city.

***

Hesitant sunlight and the twittering of birds woke me. Getting up, I showered in the blue and white bathroom that smelled of new paint, pulled on jeans, shirt and sneakers, and went downstairs. The now tidy beamed and flagged kitchen was very quiet. No sound from Mom's room above. Ming sat on the windowsill, very much on this side of the Atlantic, her eyes narrowed in distrust of her new surroundings, long tail swishing in affront.

"Never mind," I said, going to stroke her smooth, cream-colored head. "Mom might hate it here, then we can all go back home."

Ming jumped down and ran to her dish. I poured her some milk, left her lapping delicately, and let myself out into the country freshness of a July dawn. Swallows wheeled and swooped around the eaves of the house and the chorus of birdsong was deafening. I looked across the overgrown garden to the weedy field with its rickety fencing that the estate agent's blurb had grandly termed a paddock. There was an old stone stable, used by the previous owners for storing tins of paint and garden tools. Mom's newly-leased red hatchback was parked on the drive, the garage being full of the empty crates provided by the moving company, now awaiting collection.

All around was the moor. And other than that – nothing much except, in the distance, the high garden wall that encircled a big house. About fifteen minutes' walk

12

farther on was the village of Ravenshill with its straggle of houses and tiny shops. Here I would get the bus to school to save setting out extra early with Mom.

Deciding to explore, I crossed the shaggy lawn and went wading through the long grass of the paddock, feeling the dew seep uncomfortably through my running shoes and soak the bottom of my jeans. Scrambling through the fence at the end, I reached the moor. A narrow path led onwards and I followed it for a while, hopping over shallow streams and unexpectedly dropping down into a narrow gorge. I had judged the moor to be flat but I was wrong. It dipped and soared and was full of surprises.

Along the bottom of the gorge a river gushed over shiny black rocks. Sheep were everywhere, cropping the short springy grass. Eventually the path grew steeper so I turned back again to the higher ground.

And that was when I heard it; the magical drumbeat of hooves.

Borne on the wind, the sound stirred a welter of new emotion inside me. There was something about that throb of hoofbeats, something primitive and exciting. It wasn't that I had not liked horses before. I simply had not given them much thought. Now I stood spellbound by the very sound of them, listening, looking all around.

The thudding grew louder and the ponies appeared over the crest of the hill. There must have been forty or fifty of them, some with foals and other half-grown animals as well, led by a mare with a bit of age about her. A wily-eyed stallion brought up the rear. They ran for the sheer joy of it. Sheep threw up their heads and scattered with a lot of startled bleating, and a nesting bird went clapping up in alarm out of a golden thicket of gorse. The ponies thundered past in a rush of tossing heads and flying hooves and were soon swallowed up by the hillocks.

But the sound stayed with me, drumming, drumming, and as I headed back my thoughts whirled out of control. I wondered what it would be like to ride, to have a pony of my own. We had a field and a stable. Perhaps I could get one.

Arriving at the paddock fence, I pushed through it and set off across the tangled grass at a run, arriving at the cottage, flushed and breathless.

Mom was up, standing over the stove making break-fast.

"Hi," I said. "Did you see them?"

"See what?" Mom asked.

"The ponies. Wild ones – I think. They went belting across the moor."

"Oh, those." Mom shrugged, unbothered. "They won't be truly wild. Native ponies usually have owners. People get them freeze-branded and turn them out on the moor to breed. Every spring and autumn there'll be a round-up. Some, the younger ones generally, will get sold off at auction."

"Oh." I stared at her. "How come you know all this?"

"I grew up in this country, remember?"

I nodded indifferently. Mom, in her tie-dyed skirts and jangly beads, had always seemed more a city person to me. "Anyway, those ponies were terrific, Mom. Do you think we could have one?"

Mom put down the frying pan in shock. "An unbroken pony? Are you serious?"

"Yes. I mean no. What I meant was, could I get something to ride." I pitched myself into a chair at the table, seeing in my mind's eye those racing figures, hearing the wonderful throbbing beat of hooves. I gazed imploringly at Mom. "Please?"

Mom spooned food onto plates and brought them to the table. "It isn't that simple, Shelley. You can't just get on a horse and ride it. You have to learn how."

"So? I'll take lessons. There must be a riding center here somewhere. We've got a stable. I could fix it up. It'll give me something to do while you're at school." Words tumbled from my lips. I'd never wanted anything as much before.

"Are you going to see to the paddock too? You couldn't turn a pony out on it as it is. The grass is too weedy and too high. It would get flattened and go sour and then you'd have a colicky animal on your hands."

"Would I?" I toyed with my cooling breakfast. It seemed like an awful lot to learn. "You're not trying to put me off?"

"No. I was merely pointing out the practicalities as I remember them."

"Bet you know how to ride too," I said longingly.

"I did a fair bit of riding as a girl, before I left England. And Dad and I managed to go now and then before you were born. No time after that." Mom chewed thoughtfully for a moment. She had that intent expression she gets when she's about to perform a really difficult piece of music on the piano. Something by Rachmaninov, or one of those impossible Chopin impromptus where the notes dance trickily before your eyes. "Shelley, you've been very brave about the move

15

and I appreciate it. If you think it'll help, I'll ask about lessons."

"Oh, great!"

"I'm not making any promises about buying anything. Horses cost money and owning one isn't all joy, especially in winter when it's cold and wet."

"But I wouldn't want anything delicate like a racehorse that needs a lot of care. One of those little moor ponies would do."

"Makes no difference. A moorland pony would take as much looking after as a seventeen-hand eventer. And you'd need something more up to weight."

This was all a mystery to me though I gathered it was to do with size. Both Mom and I are small and slight – dainty, Dad used to say. We're alike in other ways too, having masses of curly mid-brown hair, which she wears in her long thick braid and I leave loose. Her eyes are a fantastic blue, mine are brown.

Mom said, a bit doubtfully, "I just had a thought. You'll need riding clothes. Won't be cheap. We're on a budget and we still have things to get for the house."

"Like stair carpet and stuff? Does that mean I can't –"

"Carpets can wait." Mom sent me a grin. "Let's go for it."

Mom made enquiries. She came up with Dalewood Farm Riding Center and Livery Yard – just a short bike ride away the owner, Ann Pacey, informed us in her no-nonsense voice.

This meant another expense.

"I guess a bike's priority out here," Mom said reasonably. "Let's look in the paper. There might be one for sale in the classifieds. Oh, and the piano needs attention

16

after the move. You might look out for a piano tuner for me as well, Shelley."

I did it gladly. For the first time since coming here, I felt a lift of spirits. On Saturday I was booked in for my first lesson. What's more, Ann Pacey had suggested I stay the whole day, to help in the stables and get to know the horses.

Chapter Two

"When you've done Magpie's box, Shelley, would you give Maytime a brush down?" Ann Pacey asked. "She's the bay mare in number three." Willow slim, with legs that went on forever in her black stretch jodhpurs, and blond hair cut in a sleek bob, her manner brooked no argument. When Ann Pacey gave an order, you obeyed.

"All right," I said, frantically forking soiled straw into a manure bag. She made an amused face at me over the door and went striding away shouting orders to some other misguided soul who wanted experience with horses.

Magpie was an ugly piebald with a thick neck and huge hooves. He looked grumpy, although when I tentatively asked him to move so I could clean further, he did so without objection. Propping the pitchfork against the wall, I went to pat him. He smelled deliciously of the hay he'd been chomping. I offered a mint from the pack Mom had slipped me earlier.

"Horses love mints," she'd said. "You'll be friends for life."

Magpie chomped on the candy and nudged me for more. "That's greedy," I giggled, pushing his nose away.

"Having fun?"

I spun around to find a boy watching me over the half-door, a tall rangy boy with fairish hair flopping over a good-humored face. He said, "You must be Shelley Rees. Dad said to watch Mom doesn't drive you too hard. Not on your first day, anyway. I'm Drew Pacey."

"Hi Drew." He looked older than me, fifteen or sixteen perhaps. He grinned winningly. I sent him a small smile back. "I didn't know Dalewood was a family setup. Is this a conspiracy, or what?"

"Just survival tactics. You need them here!" With a merry twinkle that quite took the sting out of his words, Drew went on to explain that his father saw to the farming side of things. The livery yard and riding center were his mother's concern. "I just get roped in wherever it's needed. So how do you like it at Rock Cottage, Shelley?"

"It's OK."

"You'll soon get used to it, you and your folks."

"It's just me and Mom. My father… he was Miles Rees, the photographer. You may have heard of him. He specialized in wildlife portraits. Dad… he died."

"Oh. Sorry." Sympathy flashed in Drew's brown eyes. "I went to a Miles Rees exhibition once. Great stuff. Have you been there?"

"Yes. It's where we lived, until now."

"You'll have folks there, then. Great. Want a hand with that box?"

Without waiting for a reply he came into the stable, securing the door carefully behind him. Deftly he forked up the last of the dirty straw and threw down fresh from the bale I had dragged in. "There."

19

"Thanks. Ann said something about grooming a pony. Maytime?"

"You're in luck. I think Maytime's being saddled up for the school right now. Take a break. You've probably earned it."

He picked up the stable bag and gestured me out into the sunny yard, tossing the soiled straw into the waiting wheelbarrow. Folding my arms, I leaned against the stable wall and looked around. The big rectangular stable-yard, approached by a solid wooden gate that had always to be kept closed, had rows of boxes on three sides and was partly flanked by the timbered wall of an indoor school on the fourth. Four huge open-sided barns stuffed with hay and straw stood behind the stables. There was an outdoor ménage and a jumping ring. Next to the rambling stone farmhouse was a paved area for clients' cars. My bike was there, propped against a post.

"Is that your transport?" Drew asked.

"Yes. It's a mountain bike. It's second-hand but it's in good condition."

"Great. Got one myself, though I seem to go everywhere on horseback at present. Mom bought in a lot of new stock at the spring sale, so there's always something needing exercise."

Opposite, in a corner box, a gray head looked out. It was a wonderful deep gray, the color of storm clouds. I stared at him. Big dark eyes full of wary intelligence gazed quizzically back at me from under a full forelock.

"Nice," I murmured, going to stroke the horse.

"That's Silver Rocket," Drew said, and added the heart-stopping words, "He's for sale."

"Oh? Any particular reason?"

"Well, he's not entirely happy with school work. Some like it, others don't. Rocket would be better in a one-on-one relationship."

"You make it sound like a partnership."

"Riding is. D'you like the look of Rocket? Want to try him?"

There was nothing I would have liked more, except, "I'm not good enough," I said. "Today's been my first lesson. It was only walking and stopping but my legs feel like they're dropping off."

Drew laughed. "That shows you were riding properly. If you'd really like to try Rocket I'll put a leadrope on him and come with you on Magpie. Just a short hack."

"Fantastic," I said on a swift buzz of excitement.

Drew brought a saddle and bridle from the big immaculate tack room on the end of the stable block and tacked Rocket up. Bringing him out into the yard, Drew handed me the reins and went off to saddle Magpie. I gazed at Rocket in delight. He was quite the most beautiful thing I had ever seen. His dark gray flanks and quarters were silvered with dapples, like sun pennies on water. His mane and tail were silky and full flowing and his hooves were small and neat. Rocket dipped his soft muzzle into my palm and blew gently. From that moment I loved him.

"Hello, boy," I whispered, running my hand along the smooth crest of his neck. "How much do they want for you, I wonder?"

"Five hundred," shouted Drew from Magpie's box. "He won't bring more than that."

"Why not?"

"His size, really. Fifteen hands is a sort of no-man's-land in horses. Too big for pony classes – they stop at fourteen-two hands. Too small for adult eventing, showjumping and so on. Otherwise he's a quality animal. Rocket's moorland bred, by the look of him. He hasn't got any papers and that's another reason for him not commanding a higher price. Otherwise he's fine."

Drew brought Magpie out of his box and tied him to an iron tethering ring in the stable wall. He came to tighten Rocket's girth a notch and let down the stirrups. "Want a leg up?"

"I'm OK, thanks."

Clumsily I scrambled up into the saddle. Rocket was taller than Wren, the pony I had ridden earlier. He felt different altogether, more neck in front, more muscle behind – more power under me. My toes groped awkwardly for the stirrups.

"Length all right?" Drew asked.

"Think so."

Clipping a blue leadrope onto what I had learned earlier was the snaffle ring of Rocket's bridle, Drew brought Magpie, vaulted lightly up onto his back, and gathered up his reins and the leadrope. "Walk on."

By the yard-gate, a really nice splodgy-coated springer spaniel grinned up at us hopefully and wagged her feathery tail. "Sorry girl, not this time," Drew told her, opening the gate from the saddle. "Gemma usually comes on rides," he said to me, shoving the gate to with a clang. "She'll sulk now, I'll bet."

"Oh dear," I said lamely. "Is she yours? She's a lovely color."

"Yes. Dad got her for me. Liver and white's my favorite. Do you have a dog?"

"No, just a cat. Ming's a Siamese, a seal point."

"Oh, great. OK then, let's go."

He clicked his tongue to the horses and we went jostling side by side down the rutted drive. At the gate we halted briefly, and then made a left turn onto the narrow country lane. It took some believing. A week ago I had barely given a thought to horses and riding and here I was, hacking out as Drew called it. I could see over the stone walls into fields of ripening grain. There was a glorious sense of freedom and a rich scent of loamy earth and growing things.

"You sit well, considering," Drew said at my side.

"Considering what?" I asked, coming back to earth with a jolt.

"Novice."

"Is that an insult?"

"Not at all," Drew said bluntly. "Everyone has to start somewhere. Keep your hands low, and then he won't pull so much. He's trying to get away from you. Rocket's got a good mouth."

Goodness, I thought. *I don't understand any of this. It's a different language.* I said, "Is there anything on the Internet that'll tell me about riding?"

"D'you mean the terms? You'd be better with a book. I'll find one for you if you like. Try and sit deeper in the saddle, as if you were part of the horse. That's it. Much better."

The sun beat down. Sweat trickled between my shoulder blades under my new nylon shirt. The economy-line jodhpurs that had seemed lightweight and summery in the shop were now uncomfortably hot. My head in the constricting helmet – the one item Mom had not stinted on – felt pinched, as did my feet in their unaccustomed boots. Drew, in his well-worn cotton jodhpurs and polo shirt, looked cool and at ease.

We went clopping through the village and came to the big house I had noticed before. White stone pillars crowned with rearing horses marked the entrance.

"Hayes End." Curiously I read out the elaborate wrought iron lettering on the closed gates. At the end of the straight drive, the house stood square and silent.

"That's the Carew place," said Drew. "The owner's a bit of a recluse. Odd, you know. Breeds terrific ponies, though. Jane Carew must have won every trophy in the county over the years."

"What do you mean by odd?"

"Unfriendly. Freezes people off. No one has much time for her. She doesn't trade locally for a start. Gets her feedstuff from one of the big suppliers. Doesn't even come to us for her hay and straw."

"Oh. What does she do for staff?"

Drew shrugged. "Wouldn't know. No one goes there from the village, that's for sure. Want to try a trot?"

He nudged Magpie's patchy black and white sides with his heels and obediently the piebald sprang forward, hooves ringing out on the gritty country road. Rocket took the hint, bouncing me about in the saddle at a brain-rattling trot, while I clung to his mane and gasped for mercy.

"You have to rise to the movement," shouted Drew at my side, and somehow managing reins and the leadrope in one hand, he clapped the other on my shoulder and pushed in time to the rhythm. "One two, one two, one two – you've got it!"

25

After a while, hot and breathless, we fell back to a walk. The road narrowed suddenly and we had to pull in for a car to pass, then again for a farm truck and rattling trailer.

"They're very well behaved," I said, patting Rocket's neck. "They don't mind the traffic, do they?"

"That's because they're used to it. Horses spook at odd things, like a bird in the hedge or bits of litter blowing about. You have to watch out for the signs. You can tell if Rocket's not sure of something by the way he pricks his ears."

On the homeward journey I told Drew how we had come to move to Rock Cottage. "Mom's terrific but a bit of a scatterbrain, not at all like a teacher. She's a brilliant pianist, though. You name it, Mom can rattle it off."

"Sounds fun," Drew said. "What about you? Do you play as well?"

"I play the flute."

He seemed impressed but I shrugged dismissively. I hadn't played much lately. Not seriously, that is.

"I bet you're good," Drew persisted.

I shrugged again and changed the subject. Do you play anything?"

"Only my sound system," he said with a lopsided grin. He was fibbing. Earlier I'd overheard the girls talking. One of them had said that Drew was a whiz on percussion.

"Are you into jazz?" I asked him.

He nodded. "How did you guess?"

"Could be the way you beat out the time when I was trotting!"

We exchanged a grin and the feel-good factor stayed

with me all the way back. In the box I untacked Rocket and brushed him down. Treating him to a couple of mints, I buried my face in his mane and listened to him crunch them up.

Five hundred pounds. It might as well have been five thousand. I knew we did not have that sort of money. "Somehow," I whispered to him, "We'll find it!"

The first hurdle was persuading Mom.

Chapter Three

"Get a grip, Shelley," Mom said testily. "Where do we find five hundred pounds, for goodness' sake? Growing on trees?"

While I was at Dalewood Mom had been at the school, making an inventory of the music equipment and getting to know some of the other staff. She had made a big effort with her appearance. Shorts and sun-top were abandoned for one of her long colored skirts and a cream blouse, and her hair was twisted up in a rope round her head. After a nerve-wracking first day, she sank down on the sofa and looked at me as if I was off my head.

"Silver Rocket's really gorgeous," I said in desperation. "Drew says he's well bred."

"Oh, yes?" Mom gave a snort. "What makes you think you can manage him? You've only had one lesson so far."

"Two," I corrected. "Drew took me on a hack. He said I was a natural."

"Drew this, Drew that! I'm beginning to wonder which is the attraction. Silver Rocket or Drew!"

It must have been a really tough day. Hastily I poured her some restorative coffee from the pot on the table. Then I tried again.

"Been thinking, Mom. I've got nearly half that in my savings account. What if I get a holiday job for the rest? I don't mind what. I truly love Silver Rocket. He's absolutely fantastic. I'd do anything to get him."

Mom's resistance seemed to crumple at that. "Shelley, I know what it's like to want something really badly and I wish we could manage it, but it simply isn't possible. Three hundred pounds is still a lot to find and –"

"I'll go busking with my flute. Some girls at school did that last year. They were fund-raising for a charity. They earned tons."

"No way!" Mom said.

"A paper delivery then. Or strawberry picking. Drew said…" I stopped and rephrased. "We were discussing ways of earning some cash. He suggested the fruit farms."

"It's a thought – I suppose."

She was weakening. I stepped up my case. "I've got eight weeks to do it in. Rocket's going to the Autumn Horse and Pony Auction if he's not sold in the meantime."

"And is Ann Pacey prepared to keep him for you?"

"Don't see why not. There haven't been any other offers." Behind my back my fingers were crossed. "Please, Mom?"

She gave in with a sigh. "Well, let's see what turns up in the way of holiday work. It'll have to be part-time. You'll need to get your experience in at Dalewood as well."

"I know." My voice throbbed with excitement. "Will you come and see Rocket?"

Mom hesitated. "All in good time. I have to get school sorted out first."

"All right," I said, surprised at her apparent lack of interest, but not eager to push too hard. "Another time, then."

Later, I made a long-distance phone call. Bryce had often proved a staunch ally in the past and I needed all the support I could muster. Besides, I was missing him.

"Didn't know you rode, Shelley." Bryce sounded faintly amused over the line.

"I do now," I said.

"Mmm. Five hundred, you say? Is that a reasonable sum? Don't know much about the equine market myself. Not the pony side, anyway." Bryce worked in communications. He was very successful and modestly dismissive of it.

"Rocket's a horse, not a pony," I told him. "He's fifteen hands."

"That right? I take it you want me to have a word in Lissa's ear."

"Please, but you'll have to go easy. Mom's in worry mode. The school's rustled up these extra-curricular music sessions for the holidays and she's been roped in. She didn't expect to start teaching until the new term, so it's come as a shock."

"Thrown in at the deep end, eh?" He chuckled sympathetically. "I'm sure she'll cope, but I appreciate the warning."

"That's all right. And Bryce, thanks."

"Just don't go falling off the wretched animal and getting hurt."

"I won't. I'll use superglue on the saddle."

"Good thinking." He laughed again and hung up.

The upshot of it all was that Mom found me this job,

on a poultry farm of all things. Right from the start I hated it. You could smell the place a mile off, a heavy rankness that tickled the nostrils and made your eyes water. The stink clung to my hair and clothes and nothing short of extra-strong shampoos and detergent would shift it.

Topping it all, the farm was infested with my worst nightmare – rats!

On my second morning I was gathering the eggs from the rows of nest boxes when I saw, running along the beam only inches from my head, a large brown buck-rat. It had eyes that gleamed perilously in the semi-dark and the longest tail imaginable. I let out a yell, dropped the collecting basket and ran, leaving behind me a mess of smashed eggs and a crescendo of affronted clucking and ruffling of feathers. When, eventually, I returned to my task, the intruder had gone and the hens had settled down again to the important business of laying. Their look was withering.

To be fair, the two brothers who ran the farm did not go on too much about the lost eggs. The pest control were called in and no doubt they dealt effectively with the problem. But I could not forget my fright. Whenever I reached into a nest box the glint of red eyes and the scamper of ratty feet haunted me.

Once the eggs – dozens upon dozens of them – had been collected, they had to be washed and graded. Before long I never wanted to see another egg again.

The plus side was the wages. The farmers paid handsomely. They had to. They would never have kept any staff otherwise.

The days fell into routine. By seven I was at Dalewood, mucking out the boxes of my three charges,

31

Magpie, Wren, and Silver Rocket, after which I groomed and fed them. Livery was do-it-yourself, so even at that impossibly early hour the place swarmed with activity as owners saw to their horses and rode them out.

At nine, Mo, my riding instructor, gave me my lesson in the school. Having quickly mastered the basics on docile little Wren, Ann Pacey, noting my passion for Silver Rocket and no doubt with an eye to a potential sale, suggested I moved on to him.

"Want to give it a try? Rocket's no fool, mind you."

Which I translated as meaning he could be a handful when the mood was on him. Not that I was bothered. In the book Drew loaned me it said that falling off was all part of the course. Anyway I could think of no better horse to learn on than Rocket.

By midday I was cycling to the poultry farm, gearing myself up for yet another hateful four-hour stint of egg collecting. All worth the effort, I told myself, thinking ahead to when Silver Rocket would be mine.

At night in bed I read horse books, devouring everything from stable management to the art of dressage, committing to memory the terms that fell so glibly from Drew's lips. Exhausted after the long day, I invariably fell asleep over a page. And cantering through my dreams went the game little ponies of the moor, the ones whose hoofbeats rode on the wind.

One evening I was cycling home from the farm, itchy and stinking to high heaven, when on impulse I pulled up outside the high walls of Hayes End. Show ponies had to be something special. I wanted to see for myself.

I was in luck. Covering the wall of crumbling stone was a dense growth of vine. I tested it and the twisted old

32

branches bore my weight easily, so up I clambered to the top. Immediately below, two mares cropped the short grass of a paddock. They were beautiful animals, fine-boned and glossy-coated, with the glow of good health about them that only expertise and hard work can produce. As I gazed, clinging tightly to the ivy, a woman appeared from under a stone archway of the stableyard. Brisk, very upright, not young, she wore work jeans and a lightweight navy-blue sweater. Her gray hair was short and curly. Her face was unsmiling.

She was carrying a bucket of feed, rattling it and calling to the ponies as she approached. "Posy! Alice! Dinner!" Immediately the ponies raised their heads and trotted toward her. "Good girls. Here you are."

I watched her tip the feed into the separate metal troughs that hung on the wooden railings. The ponies dipped in their noses and munched avidly, their long tails flicking at the flies. She stood watching them with obvious affection and pride, running a professional eye over them for any sign that might indicate all was not well.

Suddenly under my hands a loose bit of mortar fell away and tumbled to the ground with a thud and a little shower of loose stones. Before I could duck out of sight the woman looked up. Eyes the color of slate met mine in shocked surprise. She looked like she'd seen a ghost.

"You, girl!" she snapped. "What are you doing up there? Get down at once!"

"I'm sorry. I didn't mean to frighten you. I just wanted to see the ponies," I said a bit defiantly. After all, there was no harm in looking.

Clearly the woman thought otherwise. "You've no

business being here," she said icily. "Get yourself off! Go on!"

I went. But I had seen all I wanted and I was not disappointed.

***

"It's a terrific place," I said to Drew the next morning. "The ponies are really something."

Drew nodded. "I can imagine. I've got a book on the Hayes End Stud somewhere. Want to borrow it?"

"Oh yes, please."

"It's by Jane Carew. She writes very fondly about her ponies. She gives them names like Alice and Hamish, as if they were children."

"I noticed. Wouldn't it be a great place to work? Do you think it's worth going to see her about it? It's show season, isn't it? She might need extra help."

Drew snorted. "She might just order you off again! You're right, though. If you were aiming to take up showing, you couldn't do better than a stint at Hayes End."

His words burned on my mind. The book, a slim volume published by the Show Pony Association, began with a brief history of the Hayes End Stud. Founded in 1946 by a certain George Carew, the yard had instantly taken the showing world by storm and, give or take a few gaps, had been a prominent name in the showring ever since.

1946. Over half a century of breeding. No wonder those ponies had quality. Listed at the back of the book were the show champions. I ran a thumbnail down the column of names and found, toward the end, Hayes End Posy and Hayes End Alice.

I thought of that horrid poultry farm and compared it to Hayes End. There *was* no comparison. I wondered if Jane Carew actually took on extra staff at peak times. I remembered that icy stare.

Just go for it, I told myself. *If she sends me packing, at least I will have tried.*

As soon as I got in the next afternoon, I showered hurriedly, pulled on clean jodhpurs and shirt, and brushed the clingy flecks of wood-shavings used in the poultry houses out of my hair, not wanting to waste time shampooing it. Mom was not yet home. A staff meeting at school, she'd said. They always went on for hours.

Ming sat in the window, watching me leave. She wasn't yet adjusted to her new surroundings so we dared not let her outside, and it fell to me to keep her litter box clean. I got all the mucky chores, I thought disconsolately as I swished off down the lane. It was raining, a light drizzle beading my eyelashes. On the moor, mist swirled like smoke from all the hidden boggy places; the high peak that Drew called Hob Tor was totally obscured.

At the entrance to Hayes End, I left my bike, entered by the small side gate, and went crunching up the pebbled drive to the house. Grasping the shiny brass knocker on the front door, I rapped and waited.

No one came. After a few moments I turned away and followed the path around the side of the house to the stables. The owner had to be here somewhere, and this seemed the most likely place.

A stone archway, twin to the one that could be seen from the wall, led into the stableyard. Rain-wet cobbles glistened underfoot and the heavy scent of roses clambering up the house wall mingled with the pungent whiff of horse. I stood a moment, curiously taking in the old iron pump in the center of the yard, the low-roofed stone stables painted white with glossy black woodwork. Tiny ferns grew out of the crevices in the stones. It was very quiet. All the ponies seemed to be turned out, though some of the top doors of the boxes had been left open to the fresh air. Five boxes on two of the rows, I counted, and two on the other, with what looked like a tack room on the end. Not a big yard then.

Some movement in the kitchen caught my attention and I went to glance in at the window. Sitting absorbed at a big square table, frowning into a laptop computer, was the person I had come to see. Two sleek black Labradors lay watchful under the table and between them, bright-eyed and alert, sat a small shaggy Cairn Terrier. The Cairn spotted me first. The air erupted into yaps and barks and there was nothing for it but to go to the door and announce myself. It opened abruptly and there she stood in her jeans and sweater, as daunting and unsmiling as before. The dogs came bounding out, snuffling around me suspiciously and grumbling in their throats.

"Come off it dogs." Mrs. Carew waved them back inside. She returned her attention to me and her eyes narrowed. "You again."

"Afraid so." Quaking inwardly under her scrutiny, I mustered a smile. "My name's Shelley Rees. I'm sorry about yesterday. I was wondering if you needed –" I broke off as the bigger of the two Labradors came out again. He looked no more friendly or approachable than his mistress and I froze.

"Jet, go inside. Good dog," Mrs. Carew commanded, and with a doting look at her he obeyed.

"It's like this," I battled on. "Mom and I have come to live at the village. I heard you had a showing stud and wondered if you could give me a holiday job. Mucking out, grooming, anything… I don't mind what it is. I'm saving up for a horse, you see."

The hard blue-gray stare was unwavering and I stammered to a stop. All at once her expression changed and she frowned, sniffing the air like one of her dogs. "Whatever is that smell?"

"Probably my hair," I said, apologetic. "I'm working at the poultry farm for now and there wasn't time to shampoo it. The stink clings."

"Pigs can be rather strong too," she said to my utter surprise. Considering her reputation, this swing of conversation was not what I expected. "I once kept pigs. I rather liked them. Do you like hens?"

"Not much," I said, and was further taken aback when she offered the faintest of smiles. "Well, that's honest anyway. Do you know anything about computers?"

"Depends." My gaze slid past her to the laptop on the table. "What's the trouble?"

It transpired that she had bought the machine without finding out how to use it.

"So silly of me," she admitted, unbending all the more. "I just had to get one. It's all dot com and such these days and all the showing people appear to have gone online, as they call it. I thought I'd join them." She cast the laptop a glare fit to blow the works. "Little did I know what I was getting into!"

She sounded thoroughly wiped out with the whole

38

business. It struck me how desperate she must be to confide in me, a total stranger. I asked her what she aimed to use the computer for.

"Oh, you know," she replied airily. "E-mails and such. Some people have put their breed records onto disk. I wouldn't mind doing the same."

Computing was not what I had envisaged when I came seeking work, though it wasn't beyond my capabilities. And anything was better than the poultry farm.

"I could do it for you, if you like," I said.

"As a holiday job, you mean?"

"Well, yes."

She fixed me with her frosty stare, weighing me up and down. "We could give it a try. I'm not getting very far on my own. Perhaps once the breed records are on the computer, you might enlighten me a little. I would like to know about E-mails."

"E-mails are simple."

"It will need to be!" she said robustly. "What about payment… um Shelley, isn't it? Let me see."

She named a weekly wage that made my spirits soar.

"That'll be fine," I said. "Thank you!"

"What about the chicken farm?"

"I've left. As of now."

"As bad as that, was it?" Another thin smile melted the ice. "Poor fellows. They'll never forgive me for stealing their poultry maid. Very well, I shall expect you tomorrow at noon. You'll find all the information you need in files in the study. Would you like to meet the ponies?"

"Please," I said.

There were fifteen in all, not counting the foals, which, Mrs. Carew told me, were expendable. "You nev-

39

er know how a youngster will mature. Even the best of breeding can throw up faults, and that's no good for the showing ring. I keep a list of reliable people on the look-out for a decent riding pony, so there's always a good home waiting." We stopped at a paddock rail, where an ebony stallion came prancing up to say hello. "This is Marcus. He's won Best Pony Stallion at county level three years running. Clever boy, aren't you, Marcus?"

"He's lovely," I said, stroking the stallion's satiny neck.

"Yes, he's a dear fellow." A hint of warmth crept into her voice as she spoke to her ponies. We moved on to a lower paddock, where another black greeted us with a squeal and began to cavort around, bucking, throwing his head and quirking his tail crazily over his back.

"Show off!" said Mrs. Carew indulgently. "Hamish is Marcus' son. I've high hopes for him once he's learned some manners. The time he's given me!"

"You mean you break them in yourself?"

I was incredulous. Wrestling with unbroken, power-packed colts and fillies took grit and strength and Mrs. Carew was not exactly young.

"Well, there's Matthew Oaks," she admitted. "Matthew helps with the ponies and his wife Josie cleans and cooks for me."

"Do they live in?" I said curiously.

"No." Her lips snapped shut. Ponies she would talk about, anything else was obviously none of my business.

***

I did not mention my change of occupation to Mom. She'd only make a fuss, I thought. Besides, Mom had enough on her plate right now, coaching up a woodwind ensemble for a music festival later on in the summer.

Drew was a different matter.

"You mean you actually faced the dragon in her lair?" he said, setting off on a ride a couple of days later. "I'm impressed!"

"Mrs. Carew's not so bad, really. Strict though. You wouldn't take liberties."

"Ha! There's a surprise!" Drew was utterly scathing. "Will you get a turn with the ponies?"

"Hopefully, once I'm through with the stud program. Her E-mail account is all set up. She was speechless when she received her first message. It was a breeder in the U.S., wanting to purchase a yearling. Mrs. Carew turned him down flat. She won't send her stock overseas. She says you can't keep tabs on them."

"Same applies here. Once you make a sale, that's it."

"I suppose so. Just don't tell anyone about my change of jobs, will you? Not even your mom. You know how easily word gets around, and Mrs. Carew hasn't exactly got the best of reputations. I don't want Mom worried."

"Won't say a word. Promise."

"Good. Drew, what's funny?"

His eyes were glinting merrily. "I wouldn't mind sending her an E-mail. 'Hi Janey, we're just down the road at Dalewood. We supply quality meadow hay and bedding straw, if you're interested.' It would be fun!"

"Don't you dare!"

"Serve her right if I did. You should support your own village, not go deliberately trading elsewhere."

He sounded cross and Gemma, who had come with us, wagged her tail nervously and woofed. Silver

Rocket's ears shot back in shock and he jibbed. Magpie just plodded on – nothing bothered him. I sat tighter in the saddle and shortened my reins. I was off the leading rein now, though I was not so naive as to assume I had ultimate control. We had not parted company – yet, but we had come close to it more than once, with Rocket charging madly about and me groping wildly for lost stirrups while trying to pull him up. Happily, today he was not in an argumentative mood and he soon settled down again, trotting out with his long eager stride, Gemma bounding along energetically beside us.

We were heading for Hob Tor.

It was one of those moist mornings when everything looks unreal, insubstantial. The humpy, gray-green back of the moor rolled away on all sides, seemingly to the furthest edge of the sky. Mist swirled up from the ground in clinging vaporous drifts to float around the horses' hooves, so that we might have been traveling on fluffy white cloud. Sound was muffled, but somewhere high up in the yellowy sunrise a buzzard screeched to his mate.

Ahead, rising out of the mist like some mystery is-land, was Hob Tor.

"Spooky," I said, a little shiver touching me.

"It is. Haven't you heard the legend?"

"No."

I wasn't sure that I wanted to, but Drew was deter-mined.

"There was this horse witch, see."

"No way," I said.

"There was so! There was a settlement of people liv-ing on the tor. They worshipped horses. They bred them, sturdy animals suitable for battle. There were other

42

tribes around, all warring with each other. The horse witch was stunningly beautiful and she never grew old. One day there was a humdinger of a battle and the whole tribe were slain except for the witch. The chieftain of the victors wanted her for his queen, but she had other ideas. She put a spell on his men and turned them all to stone. You'll see them, chunks of rock, very human looking. It's said that the chieftain still roams the moor, searching for his lost warriors. Spooky, eh?"

Shivers trickled down my spine. "What happened to the horses?" I asked.

"Wouldn't know. Maybe the wild ponies on the moor are descended from them."

"Mom said the moor ponies belonged to people."

"They do, most of them. Some are strays that have escaped capture. They all come under the heading Moorland and the breed must have originated from somewhere."

"Yes." I stared at the hilly peak ahead. "Hob Tor. What a weird name."

"Hob's short for hobgoblin. The stones look a bit elfin, so I guess that's how the name came about. Some people, the older village folk in particular, won't come near this place. They say the horse witch still guards the tor. Never seen her myself."

"That's just superstition," I said uneasily.

"It's a legend." He grinned, goading me. "Old beliefs have their roots in fact."

"You have no proof," I protested. "It's just a fairy tale. Horse witch! Bet she never existed at all."

Drew waggled his finger mysteriously. "You'll see!"

Hob Tor was bigger than I had expected and, like the

rest of the moor, full of surprises. From a distance, the rocky edifice with its peaked summit looked bare and impassable. Close up, I saw that a stony path wound skyward, steep in places, right to the top. Copses of spindly rowan and birch and outcrops of scrubby gorse clothed the lower slopes. Through them, a fall of bright clear water leaped and splashed over mossy boulders down to the moor, where it joined the network of waterways that flowed into the river on its way to the sea.

"There are caves over there," Drew said, waving his hand in the direction of the eastern face. The going was rough and bumpy and I clung to the pommel of my saddle for balance.

"Caves? Can we go and look?"

"We'll do it later on the way down. Look – the petrified army."

A group of humpy black shapes squatted in a ring on the ground, looking frighteningly like a party of gnomes plotting trouble. I counted twenty of them. So ancient and weathered were they that it was easy to imagine ugly faces and lumpy hands where rain and winter frosts had nibbled into the surface of the stone.

"There's more," Drew said, smiling at my astonishment. "The whole tor is dotted with them. One theory is that the stones were carved by human hand. Archaeological evidence doesn't bear that out. Apparently they don't appear to belong to any known period in history, such as Iron Age or Stone Age."

"Maybe they go back beyond all that, right back to the beginning of time."

"Could be. It gets steeper here. Give Rocket his head; he'll get you up. Where's Gemma? Gem, come here!"

44

The spaniel had gone charging off, nose to the ground, investigating something of particular interest to herself. For once she ignored Drew's call and ran on, her splodgy coat camouflaged in the browning bracken and coarse upland grass. Soon she was nowhere to be seen.

"Gemma!" Drew called again. "Gem…ma!"

I joined in, standing in my stirrups, shouting, whistling, but the dog seemed to have vanished.

"Leave her," Drew said at last. "She'll turn up when she's ready. Let's push on or you'll be late, and then you'll have the Carew woman to answer to!"

We urged the horses on up the hill, leaning forward in the saddle as they scrabbled for foothold on the flinty shale of the slopes. Wheezing, grunting, they made the final few laps and brought us out on the summit.

"Wow!"

It was like being on top of the world. Far below, the moor spread into infinity, still wrapped in floating mist. Here and there, the wind-beaten tops of trees reared out of the whiteness, and over to the north the whirling sails of a wind farm touched the sky, the one sign of habitation in an otherwise unchanged wilderness.

"Wretched things." Drew scowled at the offending windmills. "They're so intrusive. I don't think it should be allowed. I'm all in favor of conserving places like this."

"People must have said that about electricity cables and pylons once," I pointed out. "It's progress, Drew."

"I suppose you're right. There she is."

He was pointing to a jutting boulder right on the topmost peak. We nudged the horses closer and I saw that it wasn't a boulder at all. It was a standing stone or mono-

45

lith. A face was carved into it, a female face, strong, primitive, with flowing locks of hair and eyes that seemed to look right into your soul. She was old beyond belief. As I gazed I felt again that strange prickling sensation over my skin.

"The horse witch," I murmured, more to myself.

"Striking, isn't she? Wouldn't like to meet her on a dark night!"

I shivered. "Shut up!"

Another ring of goblins crouched at her foot as if in obeisance. She looked all-powerful, an old-time goddess, relic of some long-forgotten religion that seemed to linger still in timeless places like this.

"Do you think it's true she guards the tor?" I said.

Drew shot me a look of scorn. "Come on! Though you've got to hand it to them, they sure knew how to get by in those times. We once did a prehistory project at school. They were a weird bunch. Spells for just about everything, healing themselves and their animals with herbs and roots, ritual worship – the works! Creatures such as hares and white owls were held sacred. And like I said, this tribe revered the horse."

"That's not such a bad thing," I said, giving Rocket's neck an affectionate slap.

"No, but they'd have taken it to extremes." Drew sat very still in the saddle, his face serious, guarded somehow. "They'd have made sacrifices and drunk the blood. It was what they believed."

There was a silence, broken only by the high call of the buzzard and the faint keening of the wind that always blew here. Again I shivered, though it was not with cold. "Let's go and see the caves," I said.

46

"All right. We'd better be quick. It's this way – yikes, what's that?"

A blood-chilling howl split the silence. Rocket jibbed and swung around. "Whoa!" I gasped, grabbing a clump of mane. Rocket went up in a half-rear, snatched the bit between his teeth, and took off.

Chapter Four

"Whoa!" I shrieked as Rocket careered down the perilously steep incline, with me bumping and sliding about in the saddle, the echo of that terrified cry still quivering on the air. Powerless to stop him, I dug my feet into the stirrups and took a firmer grip of Rocket's mane.

"Hang on!" hollered Drew from behind, amid a sudden volley of barking. "Turn him into the trees. Turn him *left*!"

I tried, yanking the rein, but it was hopeless. Rocket's jaw was set. There was nothing for it but to sit tight and wait for him to tire. Clattering and sliding, tiny stones and shards of flint flying out from beneath Rocket's racing hooves, we made it to the foot of the tor and miraculously I was still aboard. The ground was leveling out now, the mist was clearing, and Rocket, seeing the open moor spread invitingly before him, put on a spurt. His canter quickened to a gallop.

Cold moorland air fanned my hot cheeks and the ground swept by in a blur of green and gray. Hoofbeats thundered in my ears, wild, exhilarating. I was galloping. Galloping for the first time! I forgot my fear and began to respond naturally to the sharp pounding of hooves and glorious shifts of sinew and tempo. Sunlight lanced down, burning away the last traces of mist, filling the air with dusty golden motes. Leaning forward, I stood up in the stirrups and let Rocket have his head.

"Shelley! Stop!" Behind me, Drew's voice held a ring of desperation. "Pull him around! Use your reins! Stop him!"

Silver Rocket was starting to flag. Flecks of foam flew up from his mouth and a whitish lather appeared on his neck. "Whoa, boy," I said, and using my legs hard I managed to bring him around in a wide circle. The wild uncontrolled gallop fell to a canter, and then a trot, and finally Rocket pulled up to a heaving, sweating stop.

Drew came pounding up on Magpie and reined in beside me. "You OK?"

"I guess so."

"I thought you'd had it when he took off. You stuck to him though. Well done!"

"Thanks." I mustered a grin. Now it was all over a trembly reaction had set in. My legs were rubbery, my hands sweaty on the reins. I gave Rocket's streaming neck a half-hearted pat. "Silly boy! Whatever got into you?"

Drew's gaze slid to Gemma, who had reappeared and now stood panting at Magpie's heels like the well-trained animal she generally was. "More to the point, what got into Gem?" Drew said, his face red and troubled under the peaked brim of his crash hat. Repentant, the spaniel gazed back at him, her long ears trailing, her tail quivering hopefully, her big brown eyes full of mute appeal.

I thought of that blood-churning cry and dismissed the

more mundane explanations – a thorn in a paw, an ear snagged by a bramble. No. The cry had been a howl of pure terror. "Whatever it was, it freaked Rocket too," I said.

"Rocket spooks at his own shadow," Drew said dismissively. He cast a bothered glance back at the tor, and then he shrugged. "Look, these horses are in a sweat. We'd better get them back and rubbed down or they'll take a chill."

In silence we gathered our reins. We'd missed seeing the caves, I thought, legging on. Not that I minded. For one day I'd had enough of Hob Tor.

***

"Bombed off with you, did he?" said Mrs. Carew, who generally made a point of asking about Rocket. "Dear me. What did you do?"

"Hung on and hoped for the best," I replied, having glossed over small details like where we had been and why. Here in the study at Hayes End, the uncanny incident on Hob Hill was back in proportion. Animals were spooked by the silliest things. Everyone knew that. "I'd never galloped before. It was terrific."

Mrs. Carew smiled coolly from where she stood in the doorway. I had set the laptop up on a polished mahogany desk by the window. The ledger I was currently working from, containing the early bloodlines and pedigree details of the Hayes End ponies, lay open beside it. More leather-bound volumes stood on the shelf. Committing it all to the computer was going to be quite some task.

"Galloping is fun, isn't it?" Mrs. Carew said agreeably, and then brought the unhappy morning rushing back by adding. "I hope you weren't anywhere near Hob Tor. It's a dangerous place for ponies. There are lots of rabbit holes and such. One of ours once twisted a fetlock up there quite badly."

"Oh?" I stared at her, my interest sharpening. "Did something startle the pony?"

"I've really no idea." Mrs. Carew glanced at her watch. "I shall be going out shortly. Will you be all right?"

"Of course," I said. "I'm used to my own company."

"I see." Her eyes flickered over me, faintly curious. "Josie Oaks is here should you need anything." She nodded toward the screen. "Is it going well?"

"Fine. You might like to run through the data with me sometime, just to make sure I've got all the names down correctly. Oh, there's an E-mail. Highcrest Yard wants to book Marcus for stud."

"Tell them yes. Highcrest stock is very good indeed."

She left, closing the door with a decisive click behind her.

It was very quiet in the study. A fly buzzed against the window. I heard the dogs go padding down the passageway to settle down on the cool flagstones by the back door. On the screen the curser winked, marking the place at which I had been interrupted. I was recording the 1960s details. A pony mare called True Spirit had been covered by a stallion named Warrior Prince and had subsequently dropped a filly foal, Trustful. In the ledger, the name in slanting copperplate was underlined in wobbly red ballpoint, as if someone had liked the name and wanted to use it again. According to the records she was a dappled gray, always a popular color. I ran a finger

down the columns of names and sure enough, two whole decades later, another Trustful cropped up. She had a colt foal in April 1987, a black named Torquil.

There was no further reference to either of these ponies so I assumed the line must have died out. No statements of pedigree either. Odd, I thought. Better check it out.

Hoping to catch Mrs. Carew before she left, I hurried from the room and met her coming down the wide stair-case, all dressed up to go out. Hastily I showed her the names in question. "I can't find the pedigree forms for a mare named Trustful, or Torquil, her foal. Could they have been mislaid?"

"No. They'll be with other papers in the attic," she said shortly.

"Oh. Shall I go and look? I need their dates and –"

"Let's leave it, Shelley." Mrs. Carew snapped her lips together in that freezing-off way she had and went breezing past me and out. I stared after her, biting my knuckle. Why were the papers put away and not in the files with the others? And why was she so closed about it? What had happened to make her so grim, so embittered with life in general?

Seconds later the car went sweeping off down the drive. Shrugging, I returned to the study. I would just have to leave the dates blank. What a difficult person she was! Just when you thought she was opening up a bit, down came the shutters and it was back to square one!

Restlessly I began to prowl around the room. It had a lofty ceiling and a lovely old carved fireplace in polished wood and walls covered with pictures of Hayes End ponies. Some were painted in oils or watercolor, others were photographs. Head studies, full figure portraits, showring poses. All had the distinctive Hayes End look, the beautifully balanced proportions, the finely sculpted heads with small pricked ears, dished faces, and chiselled nostrils.

All were named and dated. Glancing down the row of pictures I found an old-fashioned watercolor of the first Trustful. I moved on, seeking her namesake, and came to a stop at a perky dappled gray held in traditional pose by a groom, smart in tweed jacket, breeches and knee-boots. Sure enough, there was her name, Trustful, and the date of her birth, May 20th 1972. No date of her demise though. Gets odder, I thought. No photo of the foal either, although that was not unusual. Some of the foals were sold off as riding animals and their passing was unlikely to be recorded. But why had Mrs. Carew been so reluctant to talk about them?

Trustful. It was a lovely name.

Against one wall was a kneehole writing desk with lots of drawers. Idly I opened them, finding the usual collection of old envelopes, pens, pencils, and paper clips that get thrown into drawers and forgotten. A bottom one was locked.

I rattled it but it wouldn't budge and I stood there, frowning at it. There is something compelling about a locked drawer. You just have to know what is inside. Dad had once showed me the trick of opening a straightforward lock like this one. All you needed was a bit of wire.

Rummaging in one of the other drawers I withdrew a large paper clip, straightened it out and, dropping to my knees, inserted the end in the lock. Before long it turned with a satisfying click. I slid open the drawer.

"Well!"

It was full of rosettes, mostly first-place red ones. Many were quite ornate, made of silk and highly decorated. Written on the back of each one in a careful, childish hand was the name, Trustful. And underneath, what I took to be the name of her rider, Anna Louise Carew.

According to the signature on the ponies' pedigree forms, Mrs. Carew's name was Jane Louise. Her husband, who had died in the 1990s, was Gregory. Could Anna Louise have been their daughter? Given the common use of the second name, it was likely. A niece was another possibility.

Carefully I lifted out the rosettes and counted them. "Fifty – wow!"

Fifty wins in the showing ring. I fingered them, marveling that this girl who must have been younger than I was now – twelve or thirteen, perhaps – could have achieved so much with her pony.

I was about to return the bounty to the drawer when I saw, stuffed at the very back, a small silver photograph frame. Tarnished from disuse, it was one of those double holders with hinges that open like a book. Inside, a left-hand photograph in color showed a girl on a dappled gray pony. Was this Anna Louise on Trustful? The girl's face was smudgy and I took the frame over to the window in order to see it better. She was smiling into the camera, screwing up her face against the sun, relaxed and happy. It was not a professional photograph, more of a snapshot. The print was blurred, the color fading. It could have been any girl in her best jodhpurs and dark showing jacket.

The other picture showed the same pony, this time between the shafts of a trap. There was no mistaking the person sitting very upright in the driving seat. Mrs. Carew – a younger and decidedly more cheerful Mrs. Carew – wore a trim blue two-piece and a summery hat. Beside her sat the girl. This time she seemed almost familiar, and the resemblance to the older woman was definite. Trustful – if it was Trustful – sported a large red rosette on her bridle and looked smug, as if she were saying, "There now. I can win driving classes as well!"

I moved to the portrait on the wall to compare the two. It could have been the same pony. Then again, to the novice eye all dappled grays looked alike. Quietly I went back to the desk and returned everything to the drawer, shutting it tight.

From the hallway the long-cased clock chimed the hour. Guiltily I hastened back to the computer and sank down in front of it. But I couldn't concentrate. That locked drawer, filled with secrets from the past, bugged me. From the kitchen came the throb of the local radio station that Josie Oaks listened to as she worked. Absently I gazed out at the stableyard where Matthew was sweeping up bits of straw, an intent expression on his leathery face. He was a solemn character, not given to gossip – at least, not to me. Josie was more talkative in a fussy, nervous way.

Glancing at the rows of stables, it struck me that the place I had taken initially for a tack room was never used. The actual tack room was situated next to the kitchen. So what did that make the building opposite with the big double doors that were kept padlocked?

The box next to it was bolted and silent as well. The rest were all unoccupied today. Mrs. Carew never stabled her ponies unless they were going to a show. She liked them to roam freely in the paddocks; more natural, she said.

With a sigh, I focused my attention back on the computer screen and the stud file. I must have been working for over an hour, absorbed at last, when the door opened to admit Josie. "Just got to slip out, dear," she said. "I'm short of baking things. Matthew's offered to take me into town to the supermarket."

"That's fine," I said.

"You've got the dogs for company and the alarm is on. Oh, I've made a sandwich for your lunch. You won't leave until we get back, will you, dear?"

"I won't." An idea was forming. "Thanks for the sandwich."

"You're welcome. See you later."

I waited until the Oaks' van had gone rattling down the drive, then I shut down the computer and left the study. In the kitchen the dogs were asleep, sprawled together in an inky huddle with Pip the cairn a red-brindle splotch in the middle.

"Coming out?" I asked them.

Yawning, Jet and Tara hauled themselves to their paws and stretched luxuriously, as if they had all the time in the world. Pip ran jumping up at the door, anxious to be off. First I took the precaution of closing down the security system at the control box on the wall, a temporary measure – setting off the alarms and alerting half the police force in the district was the last thing I wanted. It was a simple device and had a manual on/off switch that bypassed the automatic timer should it be required, such as now. Just inside the door was a row of hooks on which all the keys to Hayes End were hung. Padlocks are too complex to respond to bits of wire. I took down a jingly bunch marked "stables".

"Come on, dogs."

Outside, the heat of the drowsy August afternoon hit me. Crossing the yard, Jet and Tara padding beside me, Pip darting about after flies, I went first to the double doors. The padlock was old and stiff. There were a dozen or so keys on the ring and as usual, it was the very last one that fitted. The mechanism gave unwillingly in its rusty bed. The door creaked open and I went inside.

It was a carriage room. Under a tarpaulin I found the four-wheeled trap in the photograph. Before putting it away, someone had given the blue-painted bodywork a coating of protective wax and greased the axels of the wheels. Apart from that one vehicle, the carriage-room was empty. Methodically I locked up again and went to investigate the box next door.

Here the air was faintly redolent of long-ago straw, meadow hay and pony. As with the other boxes, it had a stone manger with a wooden hay-rack above, and like the carriage room next door it had a lost feel to it. The floor was cleanly swept, but the rafters were hung with ancient cobwebs. Dust lay thickly on the sill of the window with its thick reinforced glass. It was so quiet that I found I was holding my breath.

The Labradors had flopped down in the doorway, but Pip had come in with me and was scratching for mice in the cracks in the masonry. Crossing to the manger, I rubbed away the accumulated dust on the name that was carved there.

"Trustful," I said aloud.

Suddenly the Labradors raised their heads and started to grumble and growl. I saw the hair rise in ridges along their backs and felt my blood run cold.

"What is it?" I whispered, starting as Pip shot past me. Barking ferociously he went pelting across the yard. I made the doorway just in time to see a shadowy figure slink away under the paddock archway and vanish.

Chapter Five

Nervously I marshalled the dogs into the house, shut the door and stood with my back to it, wobbly with fright. Pip had returned almost immediately, so I assumed the intruder had escaped, probably over the garden wall.

In my haste I had forgotten to padlock the stable door. Outside, all seemed as usual and after a few moments I went to attend to it. Then I switched the security system back on and soon afterwards, the Oaks returned with the shopping. By this time I had begun to wonder if I had imagined the whole thing. Had I really seen someone, or had it been it a trick of the light? Entering the premises furtively was surely taking a risk. No one could have known about the alarm being off. In the end I decided to put the incident behind me, and after collecting my salad sandwich from the fridge, I went back to the study.

That evening, Mom decided to have a blitz on our overgrown paddock.

"It's a mess," she said, glowering at our weedy field from the living room window. "Just look at all that ragwort."

Only last night I'd read that ragwort, yellow and rank-smelling, was highly poisonous to horses and cattle and had to be eliminated. Our grazing sported a frightening-ly heavy crop.

"It needs pulling out," Mom went on. "Then we can get the rest tidied up. They'll have a tractor and mower at the poultry farm, Shelley. You might ask if someone could come and cut our grass."

"What?" I swallowed hard, wishing not for the first time I had come clean about swapping jobs. It was too late now. I would just have to bluff it out. I started to stutter and stumble. "But they're not set up for that. I mean –"

"It's a farm, isn't it? They're bound to have the equip-ment."

"Drew's dad will," I said on a flash of insight. "I'll ask him."

Thankfully Mom seemed happy with this. "Don't for-get to ask his rates. It'll be great having it tidy, easier to keep clear of droppings too. Have you checked the fenc-ing?"

"Yes. It's not very sound."

Mom made a rueful face. "More expense! We'd better take a look."

Ming followed us out. She had taken to being a coun-try cat and went slinking off to see what she could stalk in the long grass. Mom grasped a rotted post which promptly broke. Others were in better condition.

"Maybe we can just patch it up for now," I said doubt-fully. "What about the stable?"

Happily the stable only needed a good cleaning down. There was a roomy loosebox and an adjoining stall, with a ladder running up to the hayloft.

"Handy, having feed and everything under one roof,

61

and you can keep your mucking out things in the stall," Mom said, becoming keener. She wrinkled her nose at the murky walls that were in dire need of paint. Everything was thick with dust and cobwebs. "It's Saturday tomorrow. Want some help fixing it up?"

"Please," I said gratefully.

First we went to the stores on the edge of town and bought cleaning equipment, paint, and paintbrushes. Mom added a wheelbarrow and two plastic dustbins with strong lids. Ideal for feed bins, she said, and much cheaper than the ones from the equine suppliers next door. Having arranged for the goods to be delivered, we called at the supermarket to stock up with boring things like dish detergent and frozen peas, a necessary procedure when your nearest shop is miles away. We came home broke but well satisfied. Being positive, Mom called it.

We then set to work on the stable. I creosoted the rafters – a horrible task. Mom gave the woodwork a coat of black gloss. By Sunday afternoon the whole building sparkled.

"Phew," said Mom, pushing back a wayward curl of paint-splattered hair. "I'm for a bath and something to eat."

"Me too," I said.

Showered and dressed again in clean jeans and shirt, I helped Mom to prepare the meal and, since she had some schoolwork to do, offered to wash the dishes afterwards. Presently I heard the piano starting up. Chores done, I wandered outside. All around, the moor shimmered in golden evening light. In the distance the high peak of Hob Tor rose starkly against the deepening sky.

I remembered the caves.

Fetching my bike from the shed, I called to Mom that I was going for a ride and set off in the direction of Hob Tor. When we had come on horseback we had approached by the moorland path. The main road took me around to the far side of the hill, where there was a graveled area for parking. A farm truck stood there. Faintly on the air came the sound of whistled commands and the quick bark of a sheepdog.

Taking my fleece jacket out of the bike bag, I pulled it on and headed off along the track that wound around the hillside. The whistling grew louder as I panted up the steeper slope, where an outcrop of rocks suggested the presence of caves. I rounded a bend and there they were, not particularly big or impressive, more a series of deep hollows in the side of the hill. Disappointed, I stood a moment to catch my breath. On the slope just below, the shepherd from the farm near the village was working two black and white collies with a small flock of sheep.

"Nice evening," he called cheerfully. "No pony today?"

"No, I wanted to look at the caves. Is this all there are?"

"No." His face changed. "There's one on the other side. It's a gloomy place. You'd be best to keep away." And with that he went back to his sheep.

By now the sun was setting over the rim of the moor. Soon twilight would come stealing over the broad tracts of open country, bringing mists and creepy silence. I hesitated, wondering whether to turn back. Still, since I was here I might as well take a look, I decided, and tossing aside the man's warning, I pressed on.

Already the other side of the hill lay in shadow. I stopped at the place where Rocket had bolted, hugging my fleece about me. Quiet had fallen. The shepherd must have taken his dogs and gone. Below me, the wooded area was black and still. Ahead, outlined against the streaky sunset, the horse witch stone reared high and forbidding amongst her attendant rocks. Too late, I remembered the chieftain who was said to haunt the moor in search of his lost army, and pushed away a qualm of unease. It was just a story, after all. Tentatively I continued along the path – and there it was, a gaping cleft in the rocky wall of the hill. Horse droppings lay thickly on the ground by the entrance, evidence of the wild herd coming here to shelter against the weather.

I went inside to a deep, lofty cavern whose limestone sides threw off a dull light. More horse droppings littered the sandy floor. Painted across the walls were the primitive shapes of horses, chunky animals with exaggerated nostrils and wildly thrashing tails. Like the dolmen outside, they were inexplicably, impossibly old.

Slowly I moved around the cave, tracing the paintings with my fingertip. Despite the passage of time the colors, the earthy brown, madder, ochre, and indigo of the natural pigments used were still discernable.

Who had painted them? And why?

Presently I came to a decidedly more recent piece of work. Scratched into the rock face was the etching of a pony. Under it in bold letters was the name, Trustful. It was initialled ALC.

"Anna Louise Carew," I said aloud.

From the woodland an owl hooted and I spun around in alarm. Beyond the mouth of the cave the patch of sky

had subtly deepened. It was easy to imagine the tribe of people gathering silently on the darkening hillside, led by the stern figure of the horse witch on her shaggy pony. I could sense them here; watchful, accusing, wanting me gone.

Abruptly I left the cave and went slithering down the steep pebbly slope to the main track. Reaching the path that led around the hillside to the parking area and my bike, I set off smartly along it. As I went, the incident earlier at Hayes End popped scarily to mind. I tried to concentrate on ordinary things; how great the stable looked now it was painted and clean. I couldn't wait to get Rocket in there, to see his gray head nodding over the half-door.

Suddenly, unmistakably, I heard the chink of a pebble shifting, as if a foot had accidentally dislodged it. It went rattling down the hillside amongst a shower of other tiny stones and grit. I thought I saw movement in the pine trees over to my right – a shadow detaching itself from the deeper shadows. Skin prickling, I quickened my step, more anxious than ever now to leave before night covered the moor.

Again I heard the call of a hunting owl. The moor, drained of color, was cloaked and still. Across the path the tall trees cast long purple fingers of shadow. Branches rustled, whispering. I sneaked another fretful glance over my shoulder. There *was* someone – or something – weaving in and out of the trees. That did it! I took to my heels and ran panting, stumbling, panic spurring me on. Reaching my bike at last, I jumped on and went pedaling gladly away.

***

66

"Come on!" Drew said above the thud of hooves on the gritty, rain-wet road. "I know Hob Tor can be spooky, but to believe you actually saw something? Rubbish!"

"It is not," I insisted, recalling the strange quality of the darkness, the crawling silence. "Something was there stalking me. And Drew, that's not all."

Taking a deep breath, I told him what had happened at Hayes End and about Anna Louise and Trustful. The intruder, Drew dismissed out of hand. What I had discovered about Anna Louise was something else.

"And you say this pony, Trustful, has missing papers?" he asked.

"Not missing. They've been put up in the attic with the redundant pedigrees, for some reason. Trustful's box is always kept locked. I found the key and had a look. Her name was carved on the manger. And there's a carriage room with the trap in it. That's locked up too," I finished.

"Weird." Drew frowned, thoughtful. "I think I recall something about a stolen trophy. It was lost from Mrs. Carew's house. My parents talked about it once. It never came to light and the show committee wasn't too pleased. Apparently it was irreplaceable."

"Why?"

"I guess it was something rare."

"Wow! How can we find out more?"

Drew's frown deepened. "Difficult. It happened a long time ago. What about the Oaks? Can't you ask them?"

"They might not know. It would have been before they came to Hayes End. And I could hardly ask Mrs. Carew!" I broke off as Rocket shied at something in the hedge. "Whoa! Silly boy!"

67

He danced sideways, and then he shook his head and settled down again.

"There's old Dan Merridew," Drew said suddenly. "He would have been the farrier at that time. His son took over when he retired. Remember Rob? He came over last week to shoe our horses. He did Rocket."

"Yes. Mrs. Carew doesn't have him for her ponies. She uses another smith."

"That figures," Drew said disparagingly. "Still, old Dan might have worked for her at the time. Want to call in and see? He's a bit… well, vague."

"It's worth a try," I said.

The forge was a ramshackle place just off the village green. Rob Merridew kept pigs in the field behind the property and repaired old bicycles in his spare time. The backyard was full of rusted frames and defunct wheels with missing spokes, and the old man picked his way carefully over them to come and speak to us.

"I shod for the Carews all right," he said. "Nice animals, the Hayes End ponies. It all went wrong though. It was her!" His rheumy old eyes flashed fiercely and he lapsed into a wild muttering that was hard to follow. I caught the words horse witch.

Rob was shoeing a black cob in the forge while keeping a watchful eye on his father. He laughed good-naturedly. "Come on, Dad, get to the point, will you?"

"I am. Now where was I?"

"Horse witch?" I prompted with reluctance. Real, flesh and blood people I could deal with. Beings from beyond the mists of time were something different.

"What Dad's trying to say," shouted Rob, dropping the black's hind hoof with a clatter and coming to the entrance of the forge, "is that one of the Carew trophies was stolen. It was the costliest trophy ever, a gold figurine of the horse witch. The daughter made off with it."

"O...oh!" My eyes met Drew's in shock.

"So, now we know," he said.

Dan Merridew began to mumble again under his breath. He peered at us in confusion, as if he had forgotten why we were there, and then he turned and went shambling off, back into the cottage. Rob spread his big, callused hands ruefully.

"Poor old Dad. I'm afraid you won't get much sense out of him. Horse witches and trophies. It'll be flying pigs next!"

As if in response, a litter of half-grown piglets in the field set up a loud squealing and Rocket and Magpie laid back their ears in fear. Drew gathered up his reins.

"Let's go before there's trouble," he said. "Thanks, Rob."

"No problem," Rob said. "You might try Trish Hargreaves. She was a groom at Hayes End. Her folks lived in the village, but they moved away. Trish works for the Johnstons now. They have the racehorse yard out on the coast road."

"I know it," said Drew. "Cheers, Rob."

He dug his heels into Magpie's flanks and sent the piebald clattering thankfully away, with Rocket prancing and snorting alongside, his eyes rolling at the horrifying prospect of being set upon by marauding piglets.

"Dratted pigs!" Drew grumbled. "Can't think why Rob keeps them. Horses and swine don't mix."

"No," I gasped, battling with my reins. "Where's this racehorse place? Is it far?"

"Too far for now. We'll have to try some other time."

"Can we go this evening?" I could not wait.

"OK. I'll have the horses ready. Around seven?"

"Fine," I said. "I hope this Trish person comes up with something."

"Trish Hargreaves," Drew said. "Solid gold trophy, eh? It gets better!"

Chapter Six

We tracked down Trish Hargreaves in the tack-room of the racing yard, putting a gloss on a lightweight exercise saddle. She had faded brown hair cropped very short and the burnished complexion that comes from working out of doors. Her light hazel eyes flicked dispassionately over us.

"Hayes End?" she said. "Yes, I did work there for a while. Why?"

"Shelley's interested in Anna Louise Carew. She's sorting out the paperwork at Hayes End."

"I heard," Trish said. "Matthew Oaks goes to the same pub as my dad. They sometimes have a drink together."

"Do the Oaks live near here?" I asked, surprised.

"Yes – didn't you know?"

I shook my head. "No. Mrs. Carew never said."

"*She* wouldn't! She always was a snooty thing. Difficult too. All that trouble over Anna Louise made her worse. She took it out on the staff and in the end everyone left. She fell out with the feed merchant as well. Same with the farrier. People will only take so much."

"Well, that explains a lot," Drew said, "No wonder the village gives her a wide berth. Anna Louise was her daughter, wasn't she?"

71

"That's right." Trish began to buff the saddle with a soft cloth. Through the open doorway of the tack room came the clatter of hooves as a string of rangy thoroughbreds left the yard to exercise. "Anna Louise was OK. We were around the same age, though as a child she was never allowed to mix with us villagers, of course. Different school, holidays abroad, that sort of thing. She was a promising rider, I'll say that for her."

"She had a pony," Drew said. "Trustful?"

"Right. Trustful was a big winner in her day. They were keeping her as a brood mare. Then all the trouble blew up and for a while the Hayes End ponies weren't seen in the show ring. I suppose some were sold off. Trustful would have been a good prospect for a breeder."

"But what happened?" I said impatiently. "Did it have something to do with a stolen trophy?"

"Yes. The Horse Witch Championship. The Carews won it year after year but it wasn't actually theirs. It was a retainer trophy and there was big trouble with the show committee when it went missing. They'd have claimed it on their insurance, but it was still a loss. The trophy was irreplaceable. No one knew exactly what happened. There was this big argument between Anna Louise and her mother. Anna Louise upped and left, and next morning the trophy was missing."

"She stole it?" I said.

"Apparently. Maybe she took it to get her own back. Her mother was enormously proud of being the holder all those years."

Drew said, "And Anna Louise never came back to Hayes End?"

"You're joking! Jane wouldn't have had her back and Anna Louise knew it."

"It seems over the top to me," Drew snorted. "Don't ever darken my door again, that sort of thing. It's out of the ark!"

"Well, that's Jane Carew for you. She was the most unbending person I'd ever come across. Brilliant with ponies, hopeless at dealing with people. I don't know how the Oaks put up with her, I really don't. It was Jane Carew that drove my folks away from Ravenshill. My mother couldn't stand the strain of it all."

"Was that because of you working there?" I said.

"Sort of. Jane kept phoning us at all hours, wanting me down at the stables. Her attitude got Mother down. I stuck it out for a while, and then I plumped for more experience with other yards. I did a stint at a warmblood place up north and went overseas for a few years. Funny to end up back here, but it's just as well. My parents aren't getting any younger." She looked at me and shrugged. "Can't think why anyone would want to work at Hayes End. There must be better places for a holiday job."

I was silent. Frankly I had no quibble with Mrs. Carew. She paid generously and always on the dot. And she really loved her ponies.

"Mrs. Carew's just very… private," I said haltingly.

Trish sniggered. "Bitter and twisted, I'd put it. If you're looking for a career with horses, take my advice and stick to the big yards like this one. You get your accommodation thrown in and your time off is your own." She put the saddle back on the rack. "Look, I have to get back to work. The string will be back soon. I'm due out with the next ride."

73

Drew said we had to be pushing along too. Trish came out with us into the yard and watched us mount up. "Nice pony," she said, running a critical eye over Rocket.

"Very nice," I agreed stoutly.

We said good-bye and left the yard as the string returned.

"What did you think?" Drew asked, bringing Magpie alongside Rocket who was in a hurry to get back to his stable.

"She doesn't have much time for Mrs. Carew, does she?"

"No, but that's nothing new. Odd the way she spoke of her folks, as if they were both still living. I'm sure her mother died. Could be mistaken. I wonder if Anna Louise did run off with the trophy?"

"Well, if she didn't, where else could it have gone?" I said. "It couldn't have been an ordinary break-in. A real burglar would have helped himself to other things as well. The house is full of valuables."

"I guess. Let's trot. How's the Silver Rocket Fund coming?"

"I'm getting there. Mom's upped my allowance a bit, so with that and what I earn at Hayes End I should make it in time. I can't wait! Oh, Mom wants to know if your dad could come and mow our paddock?"

"I'll do it for you if you like. What about treatment?"

"What d'you mean?"

"Mown grass needs fertilizing to bring it on. Tell your mom I'll see to that as well." He grinned at me. "There's a condition – wouldn't mind a place in the senior jazz band next term."

"I'll mention it," I said.

"Great!" He grinned again, satisfied, and applying our heels to our horses' sides we went clattering off home.

***

A couple of days later the stalker turned up for real. I had ordered a book on stable management from the bookshop in town. The shopkeeper called to say that it had arrived and Mom offered to drop me off in town on her way to school. It meant leaving the Dalewood yard early, but I figured that if I hurried I could get the noon bus back and still be in good time for the afternoon session at Hayes End.

Church Hampton was rain-washed and crowded. Traffic noise from the congested streets assaulted my eardrums like thunder and there was a strong smell of petrol and diesel fumes that I had never noticed before when we lived in the city. I had just waved good-bye to Mom when I saw, sheltering by the clock tower, a figure in dark green sweatpants and top, the hood drawn up against the drizzle. The bookshop was situated in a cobbled square by the historic sandstone church and I headed for it purposefully, shouldering my way through the throng of shoppers, tourists and stroller-pushing mothers with small children in tow. Every now and again, reflected in a shop window, I saw the figure in green.

I had passed under a stone archway into the sudden quiet of the square, when I realized someone else had left the busy street as well, someone in sneakers, padding softly along behind me over the shiny wet cobblestones. Not thinking too much of it, I crossed the square to the bookshop. Having purchased the book, I snatched a moment to leaf through it, standing inside the shop entrance out of the rain, and from the corner of my eye I caught a movement. The person in green had darted into another doorway farther down the row of shops. There was something furtive in the act, prompting that prickling sensation that signals all is not right.

Thrusting the book away in my black knapsack, I set off quickly back across the square. Under the archway, I risked a glance over my shoulder. The figure in green was a few lengths behind, hood up, hands in pockets, following.

Alarm struck.

Plunging into the crowd on the narrow pavement, I went pushing along the main street, aware of that green shadow not very far behind me. Blindly I shot across the road directly in the path of a cattle truck. The driver blared his horn and pulled up with an angry squeal of brakes. Unheeding, I pressed on, dodging pedestrians, taking shortcuts through alleyways, anything to shake off my pursuer.

At last, hot and sweating, a stitch jabbing my side, I slackened my pace. Surely I had thrown him or her off by now.

I was close to the bus station. The Ravenshill bus was in and waiting. Mustering my last shreds of energy, I made a run for it and jumped aboard with a clatter.

"Just made it," said the driver.

With trembling hands I counted out my fare and went panting down the aisle, collapsing into the first empty seat, thankful that no one had boarded the bus after me. We moved off, chugging out of the station and along the street, with me peering out into shops and side streets, my eyes peeled for that sinister character in green. But whoever it was had gone.

Who was it? Was the stalker male or female? It was impossible to tell; everyone looks alike in jogging clothes. Nervously I hugged my knapsack to me, craving the safety of Hayes End.

There at last, seated at the laptop in the study, my gaze fell on Jet at my feet. He was dozing the way dogs do, every nerve alert, whiskers twitching at each small sound. A Labrador like Jet would ward off unwelcome guests, I thought. Or a terrier like Pip, quick and feisty. I needed a guard, and I needed it now.

That evening, I glanced up from browsing through my book in the window seat in the living room. "Mom. Could we get a dog?"

She peered at me over the music score she was transposing. "A dog? There's nothing I'd like better, Shelley, but –" she made a little gesture of regret with her pencil "– it wouldn't be fair, would it? Not when we're both out all day." She broke off, shuffling through her papers. "Odd."

"What is?"

"I could have sworn I put these in order. You haven't mixed them up, have you?"

"No. I haven't touched them."

Mom went very still. "I did wonder when I came in. Things had been moved. That photograph of us all on my desk was at a different angle, as though someone had moved it. Shelley, I think we've had an intruder."

My insides turned over. "Is anything missing?"

"Not that I've noticed. We'd better check."

A search of the house disclosed that what treasures we

77

possessed – some old books, Dad's photo studies – were still here. Mom checked the contents of her jewelry box and asked after the gold charm bracelet Dad had given me.

"It's here," I said, showing her, "in my music box where I always keep it."

She ran her eye over her collection of lusterware, easy plunder for a burglar and very saleable. "They're all here. How strange. Better report it to the police, anyway."

She called them immediately. The officer in charge took the details, but did not hold out much hope of catching the culprit. He said it was likely a failed attempt and warned Mom to make the house more secure.

She had just put down the phone when it rang again and Bryce's measured tones sailed clearly into the room. Mom launched into what had happened. "Shelley was just talking about getting a dog. I'm thinking it might be a good idea," she finished wanly.

"How about Watch-Dog Bryce?" he said. "I've got some holidays coming and thought I might invite myself over. I miss you guys."

"Lovely!" Mom said, brightening. "When?"

"Is a week too soon? Fine. We can have a bit of a break. Do you both good to get out and about. And don't worry too much about what's happened, Lissa. It could have been kids. You know how it is. The holidays start dragging a bit, they go looking for mischief. Some will do anything on a dare."

"You could be right," Mom said.

After she had rung off, Mom turned to me in delight. "Bryce is coming for a holiday. Isn't that great?"

"Terrific!" I said.

It was. In the light of what had just happened, having big burly Bryce around would be very reassuring. We could catch up on news from home. It would also be a distraction for Mom, who was dwelling too much on uncomfortable issues – such as wasn't the extra-strong detergent she had bought especially for washing my stinky poultry farm clothes lasting a long time. Skilled now at evasion, I made a mental note to pour some of the washing powder out, closed my book, and went out to the paddock to pull up the remaining clumps of the dreaded ragwort.

***

Soon afterwards Drew turned up with the tractor and mower and cut the long rank growth on our pasture. It looked much bigger with the grass trim and the weedy corners gone, more like the neat paddocks at Hayes End. Afterwards he came back with the spreader and a big bag of fertilizer and gave the ground a dose of nitrates.

"You should get a good crop of grass here now," Drew said. "What about the fencing?"

Mom made a quirky face. "What about it?"

"Needs replacing. Treated posts and rails wear best. The lumberyard we deal with has a sale on right now. Want me to get you some?"

"You might as well," Mom said resignedly.

Every evening for the rest of the week the place echoed to the sound of hammering as Drew and I put up the new fence. In the middle of the paddock we made a bonfire of the old rotted timber, which crackled merrily as we worked. I learned how to always nail the half-rails to the inside of the posts, so that if a horse thrust its head through to graze the grass on the far side, the rail would stay firm. I learned how to swing a gate and how to cut a hedge so that it sprouted up again from the base to fill in any gaps. My hands became roughened with the outside work and my skin took on a golden glow it had never worn at home in the city. Sometimes a rider would go past, and I imagined myself saddling up Rocket for a gallop before school.

My riding was improving. I was more confident, more at ease in the saddle. It had only been a matter of weeks, but it seemed as if there had never been a time when I had not ridden.

One day around the middle of August, Mo took me into the outdoor school, which was marked up with dressage pointers. From her standing place in the corner, she proceeded to put us through our paces with what she termed trackwork.

"Try to feel your horse's movement through the saddle and keep a light contact with his mouth," she said in her crisp instructor's voice. "That's it. Feel him come back to you? Rocket's on the alert now. He's waiting to see what you are going to ask him to do next. Now, as you canter up to the center, use your right rein and left leg hard. That's it! He's changed legs perfectly. Feel it?"

"Yes," I gasped, red-faced with effort.

We did some more figure eights with those complicated changes of leg, and then moved on to turns on the forehand and on the haunches. After about half an hour we called it quits. Rocket was sweating slightly and Mo told me to be sure and walk him around to cool him off. "We had a caller yesterday," she added.

"Oh?" I dismounted and ran the stirrups up the leathers. "Anyone I know?"

"It was Jane Carew of Hayes End. She liked Silver Rocket."

"Did she?" Well, we had talked so much about Rocket she had probably decided to call and see him for herself. I paused over loosening the girth, hoping the visitor had not let slip the connection between us. "Did she say anything else?"

Mo's carefully pencilled brows shot up. "Such as?"

"Oh, nothing really." I need not have worried. Keeping her own counsel was second nature to Mrs. Carew.

"Haven't a clue why she came," Mo went on. "Ann thought she might be changing her hay supplier and wanted to suss us out. She didn't stay long. Strange woman. Not very chatty."

At that moment Ann Pacey went by with a brisk, "You should get Rocket moving, Shelley, or he's going to take a chill," and went loping by with that long-legged stride, her mind as always on the next task in hand. Mo's next pupil turned up then, and I turned my attention to Rocket, walking him a few times around the yard. It was mid-morning. In the livery section, owners were grooming their horses or tacking up for rides. Frankie, the school dropout who was doing her year's practical before going on to equestrian college, appeared from the stalls with a loaded muck-barrow.

"No rest for the wicked!" she yelled cheerfully as she went past.

"Could be worse. You could still be at school!" I shouted back.

82

Frankie rolled her eyes skywards in mock horror. "Oh please!"

Laughing, I led Rocket into his box and closed the door. A glance at my watch confirmed that I had thirty precious minutes to spend with my horse – I always thought of him as mine, even though he wasn't quite – before I had to leave for Hayes End. Great!

Untacking, I groped into the grooming box for a hoof-pick and cleaned out Rocket's hooves. Then I took up a dandy brush and brushed him down. He was dry now and the dusting of whitish sweat came away easily. Exchanging the dandy for a softer body brush, I groomed with light circular movements the way the book said, un-til Rocket's steel-gray coat took on the gleam of silk. Lastly, I brushed out his tail and mane and treated him to his mint, breaking it in half to make it last longer.

As he crunched it up, watching me all the time with his liquid dark eyes, my heart warmed with love for him. The Rocket Fund had now reached an amazing four hundred pounds. "Only another hundred to go and I'll be riding you home," I whispered to him. "We're going to have fun together. And when you're too old to ride you can live in the paddock and eat as many mints as you like."

Silver Rocket made that wonderful huffing sound in his nostrils and lipped my pocket, as if to say, "Prove it, and let's have another mint right now."

"All gone," I said. Another glimpse at my watch told me it was time I was gone too. Giving Rocket a final pat, I checked to make sure he had hay and water, took his tack and the grooming box back to the tack room, and left.

The stud files were now completed. Mrs. Carew had

run through the data with me to make sure all was in order. She had seemed pleased with the result.

Today I went straight to the study to look for E-mails. There were two, both of which I was able to answer without the need to consult. As I shut down the computer Mrs. Carew went past the window with a mare and foal, and I thought suddenly of the child, Anna Louise, and her solitary existence here. Never being allowed to make friends with others of her own age from the village, not even attending the same school, leading a life that set her apart – no wonder she'd wanted to make a stand. Then again, if that stupid fight had not blown up, Anna Louise would have been here today, sharing the challenges of the showring with her mother. And Mrs. Carew would have been a happier person because of it. I wondered what the argument was about and how it could have been so important to cause so much damage.

What was the connection between Anna Louise and the cave on Hob Tor? Why had she gone there to immortalize her pony for all time by carving its likeness in the rocky wall? My thoughts turned chillingly to the tall stone with its dark image. Was it something to do with the old power? Was it the horse witch, still weaving her threads of magic from afar?

No more work was required in the office and I wanted to be sure of that last hundred pounds. Hoping for some outside work, I went to seek out my employer. She was in the ménage, very out of breath from trotting out a mare and foal.

"Here, Shelley," she puffed, passing me the mare's leadrope. "Just run her up and down for me, would you please? Your legs are younger than mine."

The pony, a sparky liver-chestnut, trotted readily at my side, her head held proudly, her tail flowing, her paces fluid. Beside her the foal frisked along, light as a leaf. It crossed my mind that next year I could enter Rocket for the Open Ridden class at Ravenshill Horse Show and Gymkhana. Size was not a hindrance in showing and it would be experience for me. And Rocket was so eye-catching, how could a judge fail to place him?

"Well done," Mrs. Carew called as I returned at a run with the mare. "You set her pace very well."

"Thank you," I said, surprised, since she rarely gave praise. Today there was something different about her, an air of suppressed excitement. The show on the weekend, I supposed. "I've done the E-mails," I told her. "And that's about it for the office work. I wondered if there was some grooming or mucking out you wanted done?"

"I'm sure Matthew will find you something," Mrs. Carew said to my delight. "In the meantime you can help me with the colt if you like. Between us we should be able to sort him out."

After two punishing hours of wrestling with the reprobate Hamish, it was good to get back and soak my tired muscles in a hot bath. Mom arrived back early to give the house an extra polish and prepare the guest room for Bryce, who was due tomorrow.

Next morning I turned up bright and early at Dalewood, my mind full of Rocket and our glorious times ahead. As I approached his box I called out to him, expecting his answering whinny. It didn't come. The top door was still closed after the night. Flinging it open, I froze. The box was empty, the floor swept clean, the manger bare.

Alarm tore through me. "Mo!" I yelled. "Where's Rocket?"

"Gone!" She came out of a box farther down the row. "It all happened very quickly. Ann was made an offer over the asking price and that was that."

"Rocket's been sold? But... he can't be..." My words trailed miserably away. It felt as if my world had shattered into a million tiny fragments and was falling all around me, and the sun seemed to go out. "Who's bought him?" I asked in a low voice.

"It was Jane Carew," Mo said.

Chapter Seven

Numb with shock, I mucked out Magpie and Wren's boxes and tried to show an interest in Rocket's replacement, a pretty blue roan mare called Chantilly. Drew was not around – gone to a tack sale with his mother, according to Mo. Grimly I rehearsed what I was going to say to Mrs. Carew. Diplomacy was the key factor. I'd be frostily polite, like Mom when she was dealing with a difficult student. Or maybe an injured approach might be better, make her feel really bad. No way would I continue to work there, I decided. Mrs. Carew could keep her job.

By the time midday came and I was on my way to Hayes End, I was so fired up that caution fled. I despised her for going so sneakily behind my back. To have purchased the very horse I had worked and saved for, deceived for, even lied for? How could she, I agonized to myself.

"How could you?" I blazed at my employer across the stableyard. Mrs. Carew stood aghast, gazing at me as if I had taken leave of my senses. A sob caught at my throat. "You've bought Silver Rocket! You knew I was saving up for him, so why go deliberately behind my back and get him for yourself?"

"Shelley –"

"It's the sneakiest thing imaginable! I've worked myself senseless over your wretched stud copies, hammering away on that crappy little laptop until the names jigged in front of my eyes, and for what? For nothing! I really wanted Rocket. Right from the start I loved him, and he felt the same about me. And now you've ruined everything!"

There was a long, long silence while we glowered at each other across the cobblestones. Then, "If you've quite finished, Shelley, perhaps you'd better go and check for E-mails," Mrs. Carew said with that rigid control of hers. "I had my reasons for buying Rocket and for now that will have to suffice. Come along, dogs."

She went marching off with the dogs padding after her and left me standing there, white and shaken, all the fire gone out of me. I felt very much put in my place. From his perch on the pump, a blackbird chirped a tune. Bees hummed in the roses on the wall. Somewhere, turned out in the grassy paddocks, was Silver Rocket. I could not bear to see him and went into the house, stalking through the kitchen where Josie was piling washing into the machine, hurrying down the passageway to the study, where I sank down at the desk and switched on the computer.

Once the office work was done I went outside again to find Matthew, who started me cleaning tack. With grim fervor I soaped and buffed, trying to work off my anger and resentment. It didn't do the trick, but Matthew commented he had never seen the bridles looking so good.

At last it was time for home. In the ménage, Mrs. Carew was schooling Hamish. For once I did not offer to help, but bid her a curt good-bye and left, walking swiftly under the archway and around the corner of the house to the drive. Once there I took to my heels and ran all the way to the gate, where I had left my bike for a quick get-away. I had not intended to be part of the Hayes End set-up any more. I still didn't want to be. It would be painful to have to come here and see Rocket, knowing he would never be mine. I was angry as well. Mrs. Carew had got the better of me and I didn't like it.

Tears of frustration stung my throat but I pushed them back, jumped on my bike, and headed for Rock Cottage. In the paddock, Drew was putting up the last few rails of the fence. He waved and picked up another plank of timber. Flinging my bike down by the solid new wooden field gate, I went storming across the grass to him.

"Hi, Shelley –" He stopped, his expression changing. "What's wrong?"

"As if you didn't know!" I said, my fists clenched and eyes blazing. "You let your mother sell Rocket, didn't you? You never even warned me!"

"Hang on a minute –"

"No! You can hear me out. So much for all that talk about five hundred pounds being enough. Rocket's been sold for more than that. Ann knew I wanted him and she didn't even have the decency to give me first refusal."

"Shelley – listen. I'm sorry about what's happened. I didn't know myself until it was too late. Even so, you can't blame Mom. To be fair, I don't think she took your interest seriously enough. Maybe if your mom had come and looked Rocket over things might have been different."

"She couldn't. Mom's been run off her feet at school."

"It would have helped. You can't expect a yard to hold

onto a saleable animal out of sentiment. You have to have proof that a sale is going to happen."

"How much proof did you want? I work my guts out at your place, grooming and mucking out all those boxes, just to get a piddling half hour's ride on Rocket. Then I slave for hours at Hayes End trying to earn enough to buy him. Isn't that proof enough? Look at the work that's gone on here. Look at the paddock. Who pulled up tons and tons of stinking ragwort? Me! And I did it for Rocket!"

"Shelley, I'm sorry –"

"So am I sorry. Sorry I ever listened to you! Some friend you've turned out to be! Get you a place in the jazz band? Fat chance! I wouldn't want to listen to you bashing away on the drums if you were the last percussionist on earth!"

"Right. Fine. I was going to help you look for another horse. No point, is there?"

White-faced, Drew flung down the rail he was holding, scooped up his tools and stalked away without another word. A few moments later he went speeding off on his bike, his head down, the tools in his saddlebag rattling a furious rhythm all the way down the road.

"Damn! Damn everything!"

How was I going to explain to Mom that Rocket was gone, and where? It was all too complicated. The tears I'd kept in check all afternoon now rose, spilling over. Blindly I headed for the stable, sank onto the floor, and gave in to bitter sobs.

After a while the storm of weeping subsided. A cold hard calm settled in, and with it came reason. All right, so I'd do what was expected and carry on as if nothing had happened. Go to Dalewood as usual and get in my riding instruction – they owed me that! Then I would do the afternoon stint at Hayes End. After all, until school started in mid-September, there was nothing else here to pass the time.

I'd get Rocket too. Somehow.

As I sat there in the cool empty stable, one wild idea after another flipped through my mind. Tomorrow was Saturday. Mrs. Carew would be out all day at a show on the other side of the county. Josie Oaks did not work on weekends, so the house would be empty. Matthew, after doing his round of the yard, would be gone by midday, home to his television and his racing.

Hayes End would be deserted. Unmanned, easy to get into. The dogs knew me and would present no problem. I knew where the spare key was kept and how to disarm the security system from the outside. Set into the stone of the stableyard archway was a secret shut-off point I had once noticed Matthew operating. He hadn't seen me, but I had remembered it.

Live for the moment, Dad had said when we were bent on cramming a lifetime's outings and experiences into those last few desperate months left to us. Well, this was my moment. All I could think of was Rocket and how much I wanted him.

Finally, cold hard reality began to creep in. Where would I keep him once I had got him out? The sheer impracticalities of the plan had to be faced. It was no good. Whether I liked it or not, I would have to accept what had happened and try to get over the loss of Rocket. My flute had lain untouched in its case for long enough. Perhaps I should forget horses altogether and take it out again.

I rose to my feet and left the stable with its shining white walls and scrubbed floor, slamming the door behind me.

Mom was in the kitchen, mixing a salad for supper. The house smelled of roasting meat and herbs. When I told her that Rocket was gone, she stared at me in confusion over the bowl of lettuce. "Gone where?"

"He's been sold. The... the show pony woman at Hayes End bought him," I said.

Mom's face tightened. "But I understood you had first refusal."

"So did I. Drew seemed to think that Ann hadn't taken me seriously. I suppose it happens all the time at Dalewood. Girls fall for ponies and say they'll have them but don't." My voice was wooden. "Anyway, he's gone."

"Oh, Shelley, I *am* sorry." Mom put down the salad bowl and came to put her arms around me. "What a disappointment. I feel partly to blame. I should have put down a deposit to hold him. Maybe we can look for another –"

"No thanks." Roughly I pulled away from her embrace. "I don't want any other horse but Rocket. I'm going for a shower."

"Don't forget Bryce will be here soon. He's rented a car and should be pulling in from the airport shortly. I hope he has no trouble finding us. I wanted to meet him but he insisted – oh, Shelley. How could that silly woman have –"

"It's OK, Mom. Really." I cut her off, afraid of sympathy in case my resolve shattered. I had completely forgotten about Bryce, when only this morning I'd been excited that he was arriving today. I recalled how I had badgered him into speaking up for me about Rocket. "Will you explain to Bryce what's happened?"

"Of course. Are you still going to keep the afternoon job?"

"Probably," I said, and escaped up the stairs before Mom could ask any more.

It wasn't long before there was the purr of an engine and Bryce's rental car pulled up in the drive. I took my time and splashed cold water on my swollen eyes. Eventually I went downstairs. By the time I got there, he was sitting at the kitchen table, talking away to Mom as she dished up the meal. Obviously she had filled him in on what had happened.

"Hi Shelley," he said, his craggy face crinkling into a smile. "How's things?"

"OK," I fibbed, crossing the room to fall into his warm bear hug. I really was happy to see him.

"Bryce was admiring the house and the work we've done outside," Mom said, avoiding the uneasy topic of horses. "I must tackle the garden next. It's finding the time."

"I'll do that," Bryce said. "A bit of digging will do me good. I'll enjoy it."

"Well, if you're sure." Mom took the roast out of the oven and brought it to the table, where it sizzled fragrantly in front of Bryce. "Would you like to carve? I always make such a mess of it."

If I was quiet during dinner, nothing was said. Mom and Bryce caught up on news and made plans to go sightseeing. They lingered over coffee and I wandered outside and leaned against the sun-warmed wall, absently watching Ming stalking moths. The window was open and the voices came floating out to me.

"But Lissa, I thought you were going to meet this head on and try to make the peace," Bryce said.

"I fully intended to. I still mean to, but I've been so occupied with this ensemble work for the music festival. With being a new member of staff, I felt I should make a special effort. But now, with this horse business – "

"Understandable. Have you at least told Shelley?"

"About what happened? No. Miles always said we should, but the moment never seemed right. We were fine as we were. Happy, you know. And then Miles took ill, and now…"

Mom's voice broke. Bryce would be looking at her, sympathy in his dark eyes. Suddenly aware that I was eavesdropping, I pulled away from the wall and walked out of earshot, the words whirling in my head. What was it that Mom – and Dad – had never told me? Did it have something to do with that weird E-mail?

Don't miss out on this job just because of circumstances.

What circumstances? It was a puzzle all right. I wanted to go back and hear more, but spying on my own mother and our best friend seemed wrong. Besides, instinct told me I wasn't up for any more surprises, good or bad, today.

***

The next morning at Dalewood, Ann Pacey sought me out.

"Shelley. About Silver Rocket. I'm sorry there's been

94

a misunderstanding. I had an idea you were keen to have Rocket of course, but you know how it is. People sometimes lose interest and with nothing being finalized I had to let him go. I wish now I had told you first."

"Right," I said, as I kept on grooming Magpie. He was in a bad mood and stamped a hoof irritably. "Come on, Magpie! Stop that!"

"What a naughty boy," Ann commented. "I must say, you manage him admirably. Well, I must get going."

I finished Magpie and started on Wren. Drew did not show up. When I brought Chantilly out for my lesson I saw him standing talking to Frankie. He didn't look my way. Grimly I moved into the outdoor school and gave vent to my feelings with a strenuous session of track-work.

At Hayes End, nothing was said of my outburst. I checked and answered E-mails and showed Mrs. Carew how to access the stud files, should she ever need to. I could not bear the sight of Rocket, munching away in her paddock instead of mine. Riding him out was never suggested and I did not offer to. This way I could cope – just.

One afternoon towards the end of the week Mrs. Carew went to town. Josie was in the kitchen baking, the radio on at full blast. It was the height of show season now, and Matthew was preparing a pony for a weekend event. I went to help him, fetching buckets of warm water for shampooing.

"When you've finished that, Shelley, you can move that new gray out to the far pasture," Matthew called from the box. "The grass is better there."

I swallowed hard. "Do you mean Silver Rocket?"

"Yes, that's the one. Put him in the top paddock. I've got to go out shortly. We're clean out of hoof oil."

Totally unaware of my reluctance, Matthew went on shampooing and rinsing, whistling between his teeth as he worked. With dragging steps I went to the tack room for a headcollar and leadrope, collected some tidbits from the kitchen and wandered down to the middle paddock where Rocket stood dozing with his head down by the gate. He woke up as I approached and whinnied breathily.

"Hello boy," I said. Opening the gate, I went in and put on the red canvas headcollar. "Want some carrot? Good boy."

As Rocket chomped up the tidbit I glanced round. All was quiet. In the other paddocks I could hear the ponies cropping the short grass. There was a spluttering snort, the swish of a tail. From the yard a door slammed and Matthew's van went lumbering off down the drive.

I looked at Rocket's smooth back and wondered what he would be like to ride without a saddle. The far paddock was only a short distance away. I could always try him, I thought, feeling a buzz of anticipation.

"Good boy," I said. With hands that shook slightly I adjusted the straps on the headcollar and knotted the rope into makeshift reins. "Come on."

Bringing him out of the paddock, I closed the gate and clambered up onto his back. It felt warm, ribby, a bit insecure. "Walk on." Rocket moved off with that light, springy stride that was all the more obvious without the saddle. We went all the way down the grassy track to the bottom pasture. Beyond the garden wall, the moor beckoned. Before I knew it I was nudging Rocket back along the track, passing the paddocks of grazing ponies. Rocket's shoes had been removed and his hooves made very little sound on the soft ground. As we reached the final paddock Marcus let out a piercing shriek and Rocket danced a bit and whinnied back.

"Be quiet!" I begged him through gritted teeth. "Good boy."

Through the open kitchen door came the blare of popular music and the whine of the vacuum cleaner from somewhere in the house. Seizing my chance, I hurried Rocket across the yard and under the archway. The surveillance system, which applied to the house, the stables, and the main entrance, was controlled from the box in the kitchen. For convenience there was also the outside control. Before leaving, Matthew would have disconnected it at the security box that was cleverly concealed behind the stone facing of one of the archway pillars. Pausing only long enough to mutter a prayer that I was right, I legged Rocket on down the drive. Matthew had left the gates open, but if the alarm was on it would still activate if someone passed through. "Go on," I said, and Rocket went.

No flashing lights, no loud bleeps. I was free!

I set off along the leafy lane, taking it slowly at first, gaining my confidence at riding without the control and security of a saddle and bridle. Once the high hedges gave way to open moor, I urged Rocket into a trot and took the track that wove through the hillocks towards the distant high peak of Hob Tor.

It was one of those dull days when sky and land merge in a mix of gauzy color. On the summit, the mysterious tall stone with its circlet of goblin companions stood out

clearly. Avoiding the uphill path where Rocket had spooked, I rode around the foot of the hill to the far side. Rocket, feeling the springy turf beneath his feet, began to dance about, bucking a little, dropping a shoulder.

"Stop that," I said, tightening the inadequate reins and gripping harder with my knees. But the action only made him increase his pace. Rocket plunged into a canter, going sideways a few strides. And then with a gleeful squeal he threw up his head and set off at a gallop. We went racing merrily over the short sheep-nibbled turf, bareback, the wind whipping past, the thud of hoofbeats in my ears, just as I had longed to do when I was newly arrived here and had first seen the moorland ponies.

Perhaps it was thinking about the wild herd that conjured them up, for suddenly there they were, surging toward us in a flurry of streaming manes and tails and the ground-shaking drumbeat of hooves. Alarmed, Rocket braked sharply, shooting me over his head. I hit the ground with a thump – still holding onto the rein. Before I could scramble up he had taken off, snatching the rope from my grip with a sickening, searing wrench. Scrambling hastily to my feet, holding my smarting hand to me, I hollered for all I was worth:

"Rocket! Come back! Rock…et!"

Of course it was pointless. With rope flying and tail held high, Rocket bounded joyfully away over the turf to join the others. In a few moments they were gone. I just stood there, alone and helpless, listening to the hoofbeats grow fainter and fainter, until there was nothing but the soughing of the breeze and, somewhere high up, the mocking screech of a buzzard.

I might have been the only person left on earth, and at

99

that moment I wished I was. Anything was better than to have to go back and confess to what I'd done.

Tiny blisters had formed along the rope burn on my palm. I was bruised and aching from my fall. First I dunked my stinging hand into the cool water of a nearby stream, and then in the faint hope that I might come across the ponies on the homeward journey, I limped off in their wake.

The herd had gone over the top of the tor. Lying in the bracken quite close to the cave, I came across the red headcollar and rope, neatly snapped in two. Sourly I flung the pieces inside the entrance. So much for bareback galloping on the moors!

Pressing on, I began to imagine that Rocket might return to Hayes End by himself. Wishful thinking, but that's when an idea struck. What if I were to sneak back and act as if nothing had happened? The problem might well resolve itself.

* * *

I was in luck. Matthew had still not returned and Josie was putting the kettle on for a mid-afternoon break. She clucked in dismay when she saw my skinned hand and reached for the first aid box, my mumbled excuses falling about her ears. I'd been in the paddocks. It must have happened then. I kept quiet about the bruises.

"Ponies! Flighty creatures if you ask me," sniffed Josie Oaks. "You look a bit shaken, dear. A nice hot drink will bring your color back."

By the time we had drunk our chocolate and nibbled a cookie from the tin, Matthew was back and the afternoon

100

was almost over. I went to close down the laptop and left. Unhappily Rocket had not made his own way home. He was truly lost and it was my fault. Guilt blossomed, nagging at me. What an idiot I had been to think I could manage him without the proper control of a saddle and bridle. Once they realized he was gone, they'd be frantic with worry, especially Mrs. Carew. Anything could happen to Rocket out there on the moor, and it would all be because of me.

My fault, my fault, sang a gleeful, accusing voice in my head as I cycled one-handed down the lane, my bandaged hand to my side.

I wanted the ground to open and swallow me up.

Chapter Eight

Bryce was in the garden, digging the weedy flower border with steady thrusts of his spade. He greeted me with a smile. "Hi, Shelley."

"Hi." I dismounted stiffly, every bruise protesting.

Bryce drove his spade into the earth and leaned on the handle. "What have you done to your hand?"

"Grazed it," I said, and changed the subject. "How's the jetlag? I see it hasn't gotten in the way of your gardening, Bryce."

"Oh, I'm great. Slept like a baby until about noon. Then it was out to the great outdoors. I've always liked anything to do with being in the country air," Bryce said. "My grandparents had a farm. As a boy I spent my holidays there. It was only a small place but I loved it. I seriously contemplated going in for farming when I left school."

"Why didn't you?"

"It didn't seem like a viable prospect when the time came. But if ever I came into some money –"

"You'd get yourself a farm," I finished for him.

"Right." His dark eyes twinkled. "You could come

and work for me then. Your mom mentioned your job at the egg-laying station. You must be quite an authority on poultry by now."

"Not really." I snapped my lips shut, feeling very like Mrs. Carew when she was freezing someone off.

Bryce regarded me levelly. "Don't you like it there?"

"No."

"Why not?"

I shuddered, remembering. "There are rats everywhere."

"Vermin can be dealt with. Still, it won't be long now till school starts. I don't suppose you'll be sorry. Pity about the horse."

"Horse?" For a guilty, panic-stricken moment I thought the game was up, that somehow he knew about my disastrous afternoon. Then I realized what he was referring to. It was the first time Bryce had broached the delicate subject of being diddled out of the only horse I wanted, and I did my best to pass it off with a shrug. "Oh, that."

"I know how much you were looking forward to having Rocket," Bryce persisted. "Have you any idea what the plans are for him?"

"No," I muttered. "Wouldn't make any difference, would it?"

"It might. Rocket might turn out to be unsuitable for the current owner's purpose and get put up for sale again." He smiled again. "Just a thought."

"Things always go wrong," I burst out, especially around Hob Tor! "Bryce," I ventured, horse witches, hobgoblins, and sacred rites seething through my mind, "do you believe in legends?"

103

"Believe in them? Well, it depends to what degree, I guess. Most legends and superstitions have their roots in truth. There's something gripping about old tales, isn't there? If you're not careful they can reach out and take you over. All you can do is try and be rational about things. Does that answer your question?"

I nodded. He picked up his spade, threw it over his shoulder and strode away across the lawn, singing tunelessly as he went. I was left with the uneasy feeling that Bryce suspected there was more to my words than I had let on.

That night I slept only in snatches, listening for hoofbeats on the moor. When in the small hours I finally drifted off, it was to dream of Silver Rocket, leading the herd with the horse witch straddling his back, her tangled hair and Rocket's mane and tail windblown, the ground trembling to the charge of galloping hooves.

At first light I was out there, making a secret search. But there was no Rocket, and with an aching heart I cycled on to Dalewood.

Here Mo met me. Her face was troubled. "Guess what," she said. "Mrs. Carew called. Rocket's somehow escaped his field and she wondered if he'd come back here. I'd have thought her place would be escape proof. Just shows you can't be too careful, doesn't it?"

At Hayes End it was the same sorry tale. Mrs. Carew had reported the event to the local police station and to Horsewatch, the body specializing in missing animals. Happily for me, the fact that I had been the last to deal with Rocket was not made much of. But that did nothing to ease my conscience.

"It's a mystery to me how he got out," Matthew said,

frowning and scratching his head. "Must have jumped the fence and skipped off down the drive – the varmint! It's funny Josie never heard him. It'll be that confounded radio. She always has it too loud."

"Do you think he'll turn up?" I ventured, battling with a fresh wave of self-reproach.

Matthew shrugged. "Who's to say? Similar thing happened here once before, so the mistress said. That was a prize-winning mare and foal. Somehow they got away and nothing was seen of them again. Mrs. Carew lost her best bloodline as a result of it. Rustlers, most likely. In those days it was easy for them. No freeze-branding like today. No round-ups either."

Gossip travels, becomes exaggerated. That evening, the whole village buzzed with the news that Hayes End had been broken into and ponies taken. Mom, stopping for gas at the garage on her way back from school, was given a grossly hyped-up version of what had happened.

"Seems it was rustlers," she said, sinking into a chair and kicking off her shoes. "Maybe it's just as well we didn't go in for a pony, Shelley. An animal on its own in a field can be vulnerable."

I made no reply. Bryce said, "How many did they take?"

"The man at the garage wasn't sure. These things often get embroidered anyway."

"Did you get any names?"

"No. You never do. The authorities issue a description of the missing animal without disclosing the name. It's up to the public to come forward if they've seen anything that fits."

Just then there was a terrific din overhead and a helicopter flew by very low. All the windows rattled and Ming shot for cover under the table.

"Wimp!" chuckled Bryce. "I thought Siamese were supposed to be fearless."

"Ming's just playing safe, that's all," I said, scooping the cat up into my arms and stroking her. Presently Ming began to purr in direct competition to the din outside. Through the window we watched the helicopter circle the paddock and move on.

"That'll be Horsewatch," Mom said. "They don't waste any time, do they?"

"No." Bryce slid me a glance. "Whoever said the country was dull?"

"That was before we came to live here," I said defensively. I stared out at the helicopter circling the moor, my mind full of Rocket. Where was he? Would they find him? Why, oh why had I taken him out like that? "Actually, I think it's Silver Rocket they're looking for," I felt moved to add, keeping my face averted to hide my guilty color. "Mo said something about him being missing this morning."

Mom was surprised. "Oh dear! Well!"

***

Rocket was not found, and once the initial fuss had worn off, things slipped back into a routine. In the mornings Mom went to school as usual. In the afternoons she and Bryce went off exploring the lanes and the pretty villages that nestled in the folds of the moor. Sometimes I wished I was free to go with them. Being driven around the countryside in Bryce's car, perhaps stopping some-

106

where for drinks and something good to eat, seemed a blessedly untroubled way to spend what was left of the holidays. Instead, I plodded through my days and worried about Rocket.

At Dalewood, I soaked up every bit of knowledge I could wheedle out of my instructor. Chantilly, being smaller and chunkier, was a different ride from Rocket. Her strength was jumping and I started on the basics, trotting over poles and then a low fence. It was the most exciting thing ever.

Thanks to liberal applications of calendula cream – Mom's answer to all ills – my hand quickly healed up. Hot baths had soothed my other aches and pains and I was feeling almost normal again. Almost. There was always the niggle of Rocket. Surely Mrs. Carew would step up the search? The Horsewatch bulletins on lost horses and ponies were broadcast daily over the Internet. The laptop was now left on permanently for news. It had been six days now, and still there was no mention of a sighting. Where was he? Had he succumbed to what was generally believed and become the victim of horse thieves? Mrs. Carew said very little about the matter, though I knew better than to underestimate her. One thing had become crystal clear during my time at Hayes End. My employer was no fool – and that in itself added to my worries.

On my visits to the cave there had been horse droppings on the ground. One evening, hoping that Rocket and company might seek shelter there, I took up some buckets for water and some carrots and pony cubes from Dalewood. I pulled up great armfuls of bracken and spread it thickly in a corner of the cave for bedding.

Before coming away, I climbed to the crest of the hill and looked all around. No ponies, anywhere. From up here the moor rolled away in hillocky waves, patched with purple heather and vivid flares of yellow gorse. I could see Rock Cottage, a little dolls' house in the distance. Farther on were the gables and tall chimneys of Hayes End within its high boundary wall.

On impulse I went to stand at the foot of the tall stone. Meeting the direct, uncompromising gaze of the horse witch, I made a fervent wish.

"Please," I said. "Please let Rocket be safe. Please send him back to me."

It seemed totally the right thing to do, and yet I felt rather foolish. This was the twenty-first century, for goodness' sake, not some ancient time when people were given to worship the moon, the trees, and horses!

All the same, I made a pact with myself. Tomorrow and every day for as long as it took, I would come here and see if my wish was granted.

After that, every morning at dawn I was out on the tor. At this hour the world swam in milky mist. I whistled and called, but the answering whinny I was desperate to hear never came. And when I gained the cave it was always achingly, depressingly empty; bracken heaped in the corner as I had left it, feed withered and mouse-nibbled, water untouched in the buckets.

Where was he? What if he got kicked or broke a leg? All the very worst scenarios plagued my mind.

I took to riding out on Wren or Chantilly, searching, searching, ranging the hillocks, valleys and flat stretches of open ground. Once I came across a trail of trampled grass and fresh droppings and my hopes soared. But it turned out to be nothing more than a party of trekkers on a cross-country ride. Another time, over by Hob Tor, I thought I heard hoofbeats. The wind changed direction and again it came, a faint tremble in the air. Eagerly I peered around, seeing nothing. The morning was intensely bright as if something momentous was about to happen. But nothing did.

At Rock Cottage I toyed with my food, couldn't sleep. Mom worried that I was sick, and made noises about seeing the doctor. I didn't want the doctor. I wanted news of Rocket.

Every so often the Horsewatch helicopter flew over on yet another aerial search. As Matthew said, with the many hollows and vales, some with heavily wooded slopes, a herd could hide indefinitely, rendering the best search fruitless.

I fretted about the deception too. Here was Mom working so hard, throwing all her energies into a career in order to give us a decent life, and what had I done? Thrown it all back at her by not being honest about… things. I was not proud of it and my ego sank lower and lower. Then there was Drew. I missed him. I'd seen him ride past with Frankie, the two of them chatting and laughing. I had not liked it.

Topping it all, I had yet another brush with the stalker.

Mom, sitting in the garden in the sunshine, asked me to cycle to the village stores for her music magazine. "Do you feel like some chocolate? Get us a bar of fruit and nut and some of that mocha truffle for Bryce. My purse is on the dresser. Oh, and we're short of fruit. Bring some apples and a bunch of those lovely seedless grapes –"

"Stop!" I wailed. "I'll never carry it all. Why not go in the car?"

"I'm resting up. Big night tonight, Shelley. It's the music festival, remember?" A pile of discarded music lay on the grass beside her. Idly Mom watched Bryce trimming the edges of the lawn with the shears. Ming was on her lap, purring. "Anyway, mustn't disturb Ming."

"Oh – Mom!" I pulled a little face, wishing she would do the errand for once. It always had to be me running down to the village. If it wasn't me, it was Bryce. All right, so Mom was giving all her energies to her new job. But that was no reason for shutting herself away, as if she couldn't be bothered with anything or anybody else. There had been the unfortunate business of not going to view Rocket, too. If Mom could only have found the time, then Ann Pacey would have kept him for me, and this harrowing web of disaster I was tangled up in would never have happened.

Mom settled back in her chair, her eyes closed, with her pretty face, which still bore faint traces of grief, turned to the sun. As swiftly as it had arisen, my small unworthy rush of resentment died. Mom invariably strove to do her best. Maybe she needed more time to make the adjustment to our new life. Affection for her welled up in me, and giving in with a shrug I went indoors to get the money.

Ravenshill is one of those sprawling places that starts with a huddle of cottages and ends the same way. Sandwiched between are the church, the school, village hall, two pubs, and several small shops. The general store was in the middle, opposite the village hall. Today

110

an event was being held here and the street was jammed with stationary cars. I had to leave my bike up at the church and walk back to the shop. As I entered, a figure emerged from between the parked vehicles.

A figure in green.

Warnings shivered down my spine. Hood drawn up despite the sunshine, the stalker entered the shop and stood with its back to me, apparently studying a display of postcards. Making my purchases, I paid the assistant and hurried out. The person followed.

Clutching my shopping bag, I walked swiftly back up the street, crossed the road, and entered the churchyard. My bike was where I had left it, propped outside the porch of the church. The follower was still here, darting between the parked vehicles, watching. Alarmed, I cut between the ranks of mossy old tombstones and went blundering across the graveyard, ending up at the back of the church, beyond which lay nothing but open farm-land. No houses, no people, nothing but a herd of black and white cows contentedly cropping the grass.

Not a soul nearby, should I need help.

Behind me I heard the chink of a footstep on gravel and glanced over my shoulder, catching sight of some-one ducking behind one of the headstones. I hurried on, panic rising, aiming for the other side of the building, only to find my way blocked by scaffolding where re-pairs were about to commence on the bell tower. I would have to turn back.

Just as I came around the corner of the church, there was a crashing sound.

"Who's there?" I shouted, breath rasping in my throat. "What do you want?"

A vase on one of the graves had been overturned. It lay on its side, flowers spilling out, the water trickling away. As I bent to right it, the stalker went running away over the rough-mown ground, leaping over the graves, vanishing into the thicket of yew trees that surrounded the church.

Heart pounding, I sprinted down to the gate and peered up and down the village street, but there was no sign of the figure in green. Two mothers came walking along pushing strollers. They glanced at me curiously and walked on, chatting. Letting out a shuddering breath, I hitched the shopping bag over my arm and went to claim my bike.

All the way home I kept glancing back, expecting someone was following me. Another cyclist, a jogger even. But the only other traveler was the shepherd from the farm, going past in his truck with his dogs in the back. He tooted the horn cheerfully and waved. Waving back, I wondered if I was overreacting. Perhaps it was someone playing a joke. Some sense of humor, I thought in the next instant. You had to be sick to frighten someone half to death.

Home at last, I entered the kitchen and put the shopping on the table. Mom was there, making coffee.

"We've had a caller," Mom said. "Police Constable Simpson from the station in town. He was making enquiries about the missing horse."

My stomach churned. "Oh?" Try as I might to sound casual, the word came out as a squeak. "Like what?"

"Like have we noticed anything suspicious, such as strangers in the area. I told him we were new here ourselves so I couldn't be sure. He said someone had called

112

to report seeing a rider on a gray pony the day Silver Rocket disappeared – you know how people do. Often they're just hoaxers. The person wouldn't give a name."

A figure in country-green flitted across my mind. "Man or woman?" I asked.

The kettle boiled. Mom made coffee for herself and Bryce in tall red mugs. "The constable didn't say, so I assume he didn't know. These people who won't open up are a nuisance. Bryce says it's obstructing the course of justice," she said, shunting a glass of milk across the table to me and delving into the shopping bag. "Oh good, my music magazine. Did you get the chocolate? Oh, here it is." Mom peered at me over the shopping. "You're awfully quiet, Shelley. Sure there's nothing wrong?"

"Positive," I fibbed.

Something had just struck me. Something huge and horribly public and official. Wasn't obstructing the course of justice a punishable offence by law? As was stealing. And I was guilty of both! *Guilty.*

I gulped, almost wishing I'd never heard of Silver Rocket. I wanted to be back home in America where I was one of a crowd, with nothing more to bother me than having to choose between going to the movies or playing a game of tennis with my friends .

I took my milk and some chocolate through to the living room and curled up on the window seat, munching and staring broodingly out over the moor. I wondered if this was how Anna Louise had felt when she had taken the treasured trophy. Guilt-ridden. Helpless. Full of remorse, yet unable to do anything about it. Life had backfired on her, as it had on me. She had lost the love and respect of her family. Was I risking the same? Whatever

113

would my mother say if she knew that I was the one responsible for the costly search that was in progress for Silver Rocket? She'd be horrified!

From the kitchen came the clatter of dishes as Mom prepared supper for Bryce and me. Salad and cold meat, quick and easy since she had to get ready for the festival. The event was an hour's drive away. Mom wanted to be there early so they would be relaxed for the performance, and they expected to be very late getting back. Bryce was delivering Mom to the school, where the support staff and ensemble members would catch the minibus to the venue. Mom was understandably excited and nervous. I could hardly go to her now with my sorry little confession.

After that it was all go.

"Wish me luck," Mom said at the door, giving me a deliciously perfumed hug. She was wearing a new outfit, one of the flowing cotton dresses she looked so good in, this one in smudgy blues that brought out the color of her eyes.

"I do. I'll keep my fingers crossed," I promised. "You look great."

"She sure does," Bryce agreed, hustling her into his car.

I could imagine her, a deceptively dreamy smile on her face, lost in her music as she skillfully put her ensemble through its paces.

Waving until they had disappeared down the road, I went back indoors and picked up the trail of discarded flimsy scarves, brightly-colored shawls, and sheet music that Mom had left in her wake. Her bedroom had the same cheerful clutter about it and I spent a few moments folding items of clothing into drawers and generally

114

tidying up. Then I went downstairs again and put the kettle on for Bryce, thinking how strange the house felt without Mom's bright presence.

Bryce was back shortly, full of good humor. There was a wildlife program on television. He wondered if I would like to watch it.

"Not much," I said. "I'm a bit tired. Think I'll have an early night."

"Oh. OK then, Shelley. See you in the morning." He took his coffee through to the living room. I heard the television click on. Ming was missing Mom as well, and sat on the kitchen windowsill, her eyes narrowed to greeny slits, her tail swishing to and fro. I stayed with her for a while, stroking her, and then I went up the stairs.

But not to bed.

Troubled, unhappy, I stood at my window watching the evening shadows gathering over the landscape. It was nearing the end of August now, and the days were getting shorter. Soon the farmers, breeders, and private owners who ran a few native ponies on the moor would be banding together for the autumn round-up. In all probability Rocket would be amongst the jostle of unbroken stock destined for uncertainties of the auction ring. If he could not be found first.

Outlined against the sky, the pointed peak of Hob Tor was wreathed in scarves of mist. All those years ago, I thought, when the horse witch ruled, the tor would have looked just the same. Vast, rugged, untamed.

Dusk thickened to dark and still I lingered, watching the night settle over the nooks and crannies of the moor. And as I stood there my ears picked up a well-remembered rhythm, faint as yet, but there!

My heart skipped a beat. Eagerly I pushed open the window, leaned out, and peered into the shadowed distance.

They came in a rush, a band of ponies, their quick hooves drumming a wild tattoo in the night. It was too dark to pick out any individual animal, but some instinct told me that Rocket was with them, and they were heading for Hob Tor. Would he sense my presence there? Only that morning I had put fresh feed and water in the cave. Perhaps they would stop there for the night.

I simply had to go and check.

Seizing my fleece jacket from the hook on the door, I crept down the stairs and, picking up the flashlight from the hallway, went out into starry night and the summer smell of mown grass. Soon I was pedaling after the ponies, the slight thrumming of distant hoofbeats spurring me on.

At the foot of the tor I abandoned my bike and began to climb, taking the quickest route through the trees. I was about halfway up when I first had the impression of being followed. I stood a moment, listening, every nerve alert. There was nothing positive, not the tiniest disturbance, no footfall, not a whisper of a breath. Yet it was there all the same and I felt my flesh creep.

Then, piercing the silence, came the shrill whinny of a horse.

"Rocket?" I called, hopefully.

It came again, quite close by. Galvanized into action, I plunged into the bushes, not bothering to keep on the path, but heading toward where the sound had come from. Whippy branches of rowan and birch lashed my face as I ran and brambles clawed, penetrating my thin summer jeans. Gamely I sped on, panting now, ducking under the low branches of the trees, trampling through the thickness of undergrowth, expecting at any moment to come across the ponies.

Eventually I ended up in a place that was not familiar, a damp, mossy place that was spongy underfoot and smelled of moldering leaves and decay. Almost spent, I stopped and fought to regain my breath. The moon was out, a full coin, illuminating the ghostly tract of ancient woodland around me, bleaching it of color. Rotting old willows rose starkly out of the marshy ground, festooned with long trails of clinging ivy. It was a dreadful place, creepy, dank, a lost, shivery sort of spot. I frowned, uneasy. No horse would come here.

Hastily I looked around for a way out. Moonlight danced and jigged, and through the trees a beckoning glimmer of silver seemed to highlight a sharp rise of ground beyond. Instinctively I made for it; climbing upwards, following the moon-fingers of light, leaving the boggy area behind.

I came out on the hillside and paused to get my bearings. I was not very far from the summit. Ahead, like a sentinel, was the standing stone. All around, the little stone elf-men were black humps in the tufty grass. Toiling on, hardly daring to hope that Rocket would be there, I came to the cave.

It happened quickly. One minute I was fumbling with the flashlight, the next instant there was a flurry of movement and something gave me a violent shove from behind. I shot headlong onto the rocky floor. Everything went black.

Chapter Nine

I came to with a slamming headache and a horrible feeling of nausea. I was sprawled where I had fallen across the bed of bracken put down for Rocket. Groaning and clammy with effort, I levered myself into a sitting position, the cave rocking and reeling crazily around me. Then slowly, painstakingly, I crawled over to the wall and sat resting with my back to the cool hard rock. After a while the world stopped crashing about, the sickly feeling subsided and my brain slipped into gear.

Someone had been in the cave, possibly waiting for me.

Gingerly I ran a curious fingertip over my still-thumping head. On my left temple, probably from contact with the rocky floor, was a smallish lump. I didn't think I had been on the receiving end of a weapon. My assailant had delivered me a shove and fled.

Why? What had I inadvertently disturbed?

My mouth felt like cotton wool. I ran my tongue over lips that were hot and dry. Close by were the buckets of water left for the pony. With great care, dreading a return of the vertigo that any sudden movement might provoke, I eased myself toward the nearest bucket, cupped my hands in the water and drank in short thirsty sips. It tasted slightly brackish, but still good.

Feeling immediately improved, I wedged myself back against the wall. On the floor just inside the entrance, the flashlight lay smashed where it had fallen from my grip. How long I had been unconscious was hard to tell. The moon that had shone over the village was now gone from sight. An hour? Two? The sky through the entrance to the cave was bright with stars, but far below the village lay in darkness, as did our house and Hayes End. Past midnight then, I guessed.

All at once my eyes narrowed on a sudden distant pinprick of light. It was moving, vanishing and appearing again, as if someone was moving from one window to the next with a flashlight or a candle. It was at Hayes End.

I tried to focus my attention more firmly, but my eyes felt heavy and my lids began to droop. Voices plucked at me, whispering. In a strange way I did not feel alone. Someone – or something – was here with me, shadow not substance, but definitely present. Not hostile either; a gentle force, comforting. Forcing my eyes open, it seemed that a slim figure in flowing robes, long hair blowing wildly, was outlined against the patch of light at the mouth of the cave. I thought she smiled at me. Yet even as I watched, the night breeze wafted and the figure fractured and became no more than a dazzle of stars in the night, a fusion of light and time.

And then I heard something that drove all thought of presences and flickering candles out of my mind. Deep in the maw of the cave was a rustling, scratching noise, hatefully familiar from my time at the poultry farm. I went suddenly cold.

Sure enough, into the strip of starlight that fell across the sandy floor appeared a large, lean rat. It stopped, whiskers twitching, looking around with small bright beady eyes. It had seen me!

Unreasonable terror overcame me. I opened my mouth to scream but no sound emerged. If it came any closer I'd die of fright. Didn't hungry rats gnaw at people's toes and fingers? Wobbly still from the blow to my head, I had no chance of escape.

It was weighing me up with those sharp little eyes behind which lurked a frightening intelligence. It sat up on its haunches, whiskers still working mindfully, long tail snaking over the sandy floor. From out of the blackness came other scampering sounds, the red glint of other eyes and a high incessant jibbering.

God, there were more of them!

Suddenly I found my voice and screamed and screamed, a high-pitched keening that sounded as if it were coming from somewhere else and not from my lips at all. Shutting my eyes tight against the horror, I strained helplessly back against the hard rock face and wished for the end.

Strong hands suddenly took hold of my shoulders in a firm grip.

"Shelley! It's all right! Stop it! It's me, Drew!"

I opened my eyes and looked, incredibly, into Drew's baffled face.

"I… I saw rats!" I wailed, quaking from head to foot. "Lots of them! They were coming for me! Oh, it was h…horrible!"

Tears spurted, streaming down my cheeks. I sobbed and sobbed and could not stop shaking. Through a haze of shock I felt Drew's arms come around me in a comforting hug, and heard his voice soothing. "It's all right, Shelley. They've gone now and I'm here with you. Everything's fine. Look, you've had a scare. Take it easy for a while. Then you can tell me what this is all about."

Settling down beside me on the straw, he gently eased my still-pounding head onto his shoulder. Gratefully, I leaned against him until the trembling ceased and the pain in my head faded a little. Puzzled now as to why Drew was here, I sat up and again ran an exploratory fingertip over my forehead, wincing. "Ouch!"

"Quite a bump there," Drew said. "D'you feel like telling me what happened?"

"Someone shoved me and I fell and struck my head," I said dully. "But what about you? How come you're wandering around on the moor at this hour? It's got to be the middle of the night."

"It is. I was on my way to bed when I saw a light at Hayes End. It looked a bit fishy. Mom and Dad had gone out for a meal with friends and they're always late getting back, so I decided not to hang about. I tacked up Magpie and rode over there."

"And?"

"The place was in darkness. Not a squeak out of the dogs. She's got security lights there, hasn't she? They weren't operating."

"There aren't any lights in the attic," I said. "Josie Oaks always leaves candles there, just in case they're needed. Maybe Mrs. Carew went up there for something."

"Mmm." Drew sounded dubious. "Anyway, everything seemed OK so I left. I decided to take the quick route home across the moor. We were passing the tor when I heard you yelling fit to raise the dead. Magpie nearly took off in fright."

"Sorry."

"Don't be. I'm just glad I was around. D'you feel strong enough to ride? I guess Magpie can manage the two of us. What a night! You can tell me more about what you were doing messing around here as we go."

He helped me up and we went out into the cool starlit night, where dear old Magpie waited with a faintly be-mused expression on his patchy face. Drew mounted, hauling me up behind him. We set off at a steady walk, my arms tight around Drew's waist. As we rode, I spoke about my search for the pony herd.

"It was freaky," I said, shuddering. "I went at it like someone demented. It was like I was being driven by some force outside my control. I ended up in this swamp and –"

"There is no swamp on Hob Tor," Drew cut in.

"But I was there, I tell you. The ground was all soggy and the trees were dead-looking and covered in lichen. It stank too. It smelled of death and decay. It was a vile place. It was… sort of… unreal."

Drew was silent, yet his rigid shoulders and the stern way he held his head spoke volumes. He knew what I was talking about all right, only he was not admitting to it. Only girls got freaked out by other-world experiences. Boys either denied the fact that they happened or kept quiet about it.

If my hunch was correct and time had slipped, whisk-ing me back to that perilous age of warring tribes and rit-ual slaughter, then what of that other incident in the

123

cave? Bizarre though it seemed, the half-dreamed impression of a figure outlined against the night sky had been a comfort. Had there truly been someone there? Some protective force, conjured up out of the night by my imagination and fear? Or had I simply dreamed it? I could have been hallucinating. That had been some crack to the head!

"Anyway," I went on wearily, "the ponies were nowhere to be seen and I carried on up the hill to the cave. You know the rest."

We rode on in silence, the cool night air fanning my hot cheeks and lulling the pain in my head to a dull ache. Roughly halfway to Hayes End, Drew said urgently, "Look, up in the attic! That light again!" He reined Magpie in and we watched, curious, as the dancing flame came and went at the windows. "Weird," Drew said. "What's going on?"

"Don't know." My head was starting to throb again. All I wanted was home, some painkillers, and my bed.

"I don't like it," said Drew. "I'm taking a closer look."

Before I could protest he had legged Magpie into a sharp canter. Wincing at every jolt, I buried my face in Drew's back and focused on keeping my balance. We reined in by the garden wall. Unexpectedly, out of the darkness came a tentative huffle of greeting. Tethered under the trees, a dark shape in the shadows, was a tall bay horse.

"Gets weirder," Drew whispered over his shoulder. "You stay here with Magpie. I'm going in."

He swung his leg forward over the horse's neck and dropped silently down onto the grass.

"I'm coming with you," I said, dismounting with more

124

haste than was good for my paining head. No way was I going to be left here on my own.

"OK. Keep close to me and keep quiet. I'll tie Magpie up."

"Any idea who that horse belongs to?"

"No. And I said keep quiet."

Staying on the grass, we crept around to the front gates and found them closed against the night. Returning to the ivy-covered wall, we entered that way, clambering up the branches and dropping down the other side into the soft earth of the shrubbery. Drew put a warning finger to his lips, then indicated that I should lead the way. I went cautiously, unnerved by the uneasy silence and the lack of the halogen lights that normally rendered the stableyard bright as day.

We passed under the archway and heard a muffled barking from the stables. "Never mind them," Drew mouthed, pointing to the kitchen door, which was open. "Me first."

In the kitchen, the wood-burning stove was cold. The place was still and lifeless. Easing open the door, we stole along the silent passageway, glancing into each room as we went. All were empty, deserted. At the foot of the stairway we halted. Listened. A sound from a floor above, so faint it might have been imagined, made us stiffen. Drew silently gestured his intent to go and investigate. I shook my head, pointing instead to the telephone on the hall table.

"Police," I mouthed.

We tried but the line was dead. There was nothing for it but to keep going. Where was Mrs. Carew? Why this awful, weighty silence? My mind offered up answers all too readily and at that moment I felt sorry to have crossed her. Difficult and domineering she might be, but she was no longer young and she was all alone in the world. In her autocratic way, and aside from Rocket, she had been good to me. Please let her be all right, I prayed as I stealthily followed Drew up the sweeping flight of stairs to the landing.

The sound came again, a thud as if someone had closed a heavy lid on a box or chest. It came from above. As we crossed the landing, our footsteps muffled by the thick wool carpet on the floor, Drew silently indicated the narrow passageway to the attic, at the end of which a faint light glimmered. Cautiously we entered the corridor. At the end, the solid door that was always kept shut and bolted, stood open.

Hardly daring to draw breath, we crept up the steep attic stair. The door at the top was also ajar. Moonlight gleamed in through the small dormer windows of the shadowy roof spaces, and in its beam and that of the flickering candle on the floor, a dark-clad figure could be seen bent over a large wooden chest. Other boxes stood open and ransacked. The floor was littered with screwed up bits of paper, old books and toys, and long-discarded moth-eaten curtains. The debris of decades of family life had been stowed away up here and was now thrown randomly about in the intruder's search for – what?

Under Drew's foot, a floorboard suddenly creaked. The intruder's head shot up, and a pair of very startled light hazel eyes regarded us from a wind-burnished face.

"You!" I gasped.

Chapter Ten

Trish Hargreaves abandoned the wooden chest she was sifting through and stood up, her face scowling in the candlelight. "What are you two doing here?" she said nastily.

"We could ask you the same," Drew said, drawing me into the room and closing the door behind us. "Dogs shut away, owner nowhere to be seen, phone disconnected, and now this." A sweep of his hand embraced the plundered attic. "What's it all about, Trish?"

She shrugged. "OK. I was looking for something. Didn't want to be disturbed."

"No kidding," I said furiously. "Looking for trouble, more than likely! It was you up at the cave, wasn't it?"

"What if it was," she retorted, sulky.

"What about the stalking? Was that you as well?"

"I had to keep an eye on you, didn't I? Coming here asking questions, stirring things up. I guessed you were trouble the first time I saw you, Shelley Rees. I was out riding by the tor. You'd been poking around the cave then."

"I'd biked up there. You gave me a fright."

"Tough!"

"But why me?" I cried. "What have I done?"

Drew gave me a surreptitious nudge. Careful, it inferred. Leave this to me. He said, coaxing, "Come on, Trish. Tell us what you're really doing here."

Trish's manner abruptly changed, hostile defense giving way to an oddly disturbing childlike simper, rather like watching an actor playing two totally contrasting roles. "If you must know, I came to return something," Trish said.

"Oh yes?" Drew held her gaze levelly. "Return what?"

"The Horse Witch Trophy. Call it conscience if you like."

Silence. Then, "I think," Drew said slowly, "that you'd better explain."

She shrugged again, the old Trish once more, the Trish I knew. I stared at her in horrified fascination. Plainly something here was very, very wrong.

"Guess I've got nothing to lose," Trish said. "It all started when I was a groom here. Anna Louise and I were around the same age. We got sort of chummy – well, she didn't have that many friends. Had everything else though – looks, brains, wealth, any horse she wanted. Wasn't enough for Anna Louise. She had to go and steal my boyfriend as well."

So that was it. Jealousy, pure and simple. Drew groaned. "Come on, Trish!"

"Well, there I was working like a dog for pittance, and she had to barge in on the one area of my life that was going well. He was a great guy. We were getting along just fine, though thinking about it now, we probably wouldn't have lasted. He was more Anna Louise's type than mine. But at the time it hurt. He wasn't good enough for the Carews, being an American and all. Of course, old lady Carew wouldn't have liked anyone coming to steal away her precious daughter. There was a humdinger of a fight about him and Anna Louise upped and left. I thought since she was in for it anyway, a bit more mud wouldn't matter. And there was that trophy, left on the shelf in the study just asking to be stolen."

"So you took it and threw the blame on Anna Louise," Drew said.

"What did you do with the trophy?" I asked. I knew, I just knew what the answer would be.

"Hid it in the cave on Hob Tor," Trish answered. "Anna Louise had a thing about that place. She told me she once saw the horse witch there. Her pony had gone badly lame and she asked for a spell for it to be cured."

"Did it work?" I wanted to know.

"Of course it worked. The pony recovered. The vet had all but given up on it." Trish shuddered. "Ugh, that cave! No one goes there much, so I knew the trophy would be safe. Anyway, it seemed right to let the horse witch guard it."

"You really believe in the legend?" I said.

Trish cast me a pitying look. "Doesn't everyone? Ask the villagers, they'll tell you! The horse witch is all powerful. You bet I believe in her!" She went suddenly very still, her eyes wide and scared yet shining with a strange hard light. "That's why I couldn't move the trophy before," she continued in a frightened whisper. "I was afraid of what she might do. She'd have taken her revenge. She's like that. Spiteful."

"But you've gone ahead and moved the trophy now –" Drew prompted.

"Had to, didn't I?" The glittery eyes moved shiftily to me. "When Shelley started snooping around up at the tor I was worried she'd find the trophy and my secret would be out. There are ways of tracing people. Fingerprints, data-bases. My prints would have been all over it. The attic at Hayes End, I thought. That's where I'll put it. It's out of my hands then. Out of my hands!"

At that moment the mask that had concealed the mental instability that must have been there all along, slipped for good. Trish looked wild, unpredictable, dangerous. I felt scared. Scared for myself and for Drew, shut away up here with madness. I wanted to be gone and threw a longing look at the door. Drew though, wanted more explanations.

"Doesn't make sense," he said. "You'd got away with the theft. Why didn't you simply stay away from here? Why come back?"

"Had to. It was her, the horse witch. She made me come back. First thing I did when I came back here was visit the cave and pacify her. I brought her nice things. Paid homage. She left me alone after that. There'd been changes at Hayes End in my absence. Mr. Carew had died. He wasn't a bad old guy. I quite liked him. It was the old girl I hated."

"Mrs. Carew's all right," I said spiritedly in her defense.

Trish curled a lip. "Well, you would think that."

"What d'you mean?" I said.

"Shelley!" Drew shot me a silencing glance. "Trish, about this trophy. Weren't you taking a risk bringing it back here?"

"Not really. Getting in was no problem. I knew about the hidden security box, and the dogs were easily dealt with. So was the old girl. Shelley was the problem, al-

131

ways popping up when I least expected it. I'd sussed out the place when I thought everyone was out –"

"So that was you as well!" I said.

"Yeah, me! But you were fooling around in the stables. I had to change my tactics after that. There was the pony that went missing as well. I had an idea you might be behind it. I thought you had him hidden away somewhere. I heard how upset you were when he was sold."

"Would I do a fool thing like that?" I muttered.

"You might. It's a good pony. Anyway, earlier I was riding on the moor when the wild herd went by. I saw you leave your house and bike off after them. I thought you might lead me to the pony and decided to follow. Lost you for a while, you just vanished. I went on to the cave and checked that the trophy was still where I'd left it, in a cleft in the rock right at the back. Did you know there's a colony of bats living there?"

"Rats too," I said, quaking in remembered horror.

"That's no surprise. There's a secret chamber. It was excavated once, but so much went wrong – unexplained accidents, children having nightmares, that sort of thing – they sealed it up again."

"Trish!" Drew said, exasperated. "Keep to the point."

"There isn't much more to tell," Trish said, "When I saw the bracken and feed buckets, I thought I was right about the pony and decided to wait for a while. It seemed like ages before Shelley turned up."

"It was that swampy place. I couldn't find a way out."

"I told you," Drew said with wearied patience. "There is no swamp on Hob Tor."

Trish laughed hollowly. "Oh, isn't there! I'd believe anything of Hob Tor and so do you Drew Pacey, deep down!"

132

"Someone was there, following me," I insisted.

"Well it wasn't me." Trish swallowed hard. "Grief, that cave! It really freaked me out. Tonight there was something else there, something dark – oh, I don't know. I just wanted to get away. Then Shelley appeared and I panicked."

I gnawed my lip, thinking. Someone in that inhospitable tract of woodland had been on my tail. If it wasn't Trish, then who had it been? Was it the chieftain who was said to haunt the moor? I recalled the glancing moonlight, shining like a beacon through the trees. And the whinnying horse, the creepy feeling of being lost in a place that was totally alien – and suddenly I understood.

It had been her all along, the horse witch. Of course there was no swamp on Hob Tor, not any more. But there had once been. Unlike poor mad Trish, the horse witch was on my side. A good force, protecting, guiding me safely out of it.

"So you clobbered Shelley and left her to her fate." Drew shook his head sorrowfully. "Nice!"

"She survived. I suppose I could have done it another way. I suppose Shelley wouldn't have said anything. There's this iffy business over the pony. If she's got him hidden away as I suspect, we could have struck a bargain. Her silence for mine." Trish paused.

I said, "I haven't got him. Truly."

"Of course Shelley hasn't," Drew said. "So you brought the trophy here and hid it. Then you hung around. What else were you up to, Trish?"

"That's my business," she replied.

"The police aren't going to like it," Drew said on a warning note. "What have you done to Mrs. Carew?"

"Find out for yourself!"

I'd heard enough! With a cry of protest I flew at her. Trish flung me off as if I were no more than a bit of fluff. I landed against the wooden chest, scattering papers in all directions. Drew dived to the rescue and Trish gave him a karate chop across his chest, felling him. She bounded for the door, wrenched it open, and was gone. Struggling up, both of us gasping, we heard her pounding down the wooden stairs to the bottom. The landing door closed with a crash.

"After her!" Drew rasped, clutching his ribs.

We went stumbling off down the steps in pursuit. The door refused to budge. "She's locked it!" Drew said, ramming his shoulder into it. I joined him, pushing, but the solid wooden door did not give an inch. "She'll get away! Damn!"

Frantically I rattled the latch. "We've got to get out of here. We've got to find Mrs. Carew." I stopped, sniffing. "Drew, can you smell something?"

Even as I spoke, down the stairwell came a faint curl of smoke. "The candle!" Drew gasped. "It must have got knocked over. It's started a fire. Quick, we have to stamp it out."

Already it was too late. The scattered paper had caught and the flames were spreading, licking up around the center floor struts of ancient timber, sending out clouds of smoke. Drew tore off his shirt and flung it at me.

"Put it over your face!" he said, coughing. He yanked a handkerchief out of his jodhpur pocket and held to his own face. "Is there any other way out?"

"Only the window."

"Too far to jump. Is there another exit? Think, Shelley!"

135

"I'm trying to. I don't know!" I was beginning to panic. Part of the attic was sectioned off, probably decades ago when the plumbing was installed. "Wait. There's a loft! There might be a trapdoor into it."

It was on the far side of the attic, away from the growing fire. Seizing my hand, Drew dragged me over the creaky floor to the low door set into the dividing wall. He hurled it open. "Go on!"

Inside, Drew shut the door with a slam, pitching us into darkness. "No window," Drew muttered. "I can't see a thing, can you?"

"Not yet." I yanked the covering from my mouth and nose and gratefully gasped in great lungfuls of musty but smoke-free air. Not for long though. The wooden partition was thin. Once the fire had reached it, the wall would go up like tinder. We were trapped!

Around us was the plip-plop of water. "The cold-water tank for the house must be here somewhere," said Drew, lumbering blindly about. "Ouch, my shin! Here it is. Should be open-topped. Yes. Pass me that shirt. I'll dunk it in the water. We should dunk ourselves too. Go on, get really wet. Don't forget your hair."

We drenched ourselves thoroughly, after which Drew scooped up hasty handfuls and chucked it at the wooden partition. We both knew the action was futile. Hoses and fire fighting foam were what we needed, not paltry splashes of water. By now our eyes were getting used to the lack of light. Dim shapes presented themselves, looming up out of the darkness. Water pipes snaked overhead and down the walls, disappearing into the floor below.

"Look," I said, pointing. Where the pipes went

136

through there was quite a gap. "If we're where I think we are, there's a walk-in cupboard below us where Josie keeps her cleaning things. We only have to ease up another floorboard and we can get out."

"Good thinking!"

We pulled and stamped, but the long-seasoned wood was as hard as flint and would not give.

"We need a lever. A bit of spare piping would do," Drew said.

Dripping water everywhere, we scratched frantically around for a likely object among the dust and mouse droppings on the floor. Finding nothing, I darted back to the outlet space. "It's narrow but I'm thin. I might just get through. I think Matthew keeps a spare toolbox there. There's sure to be something in it we could use."

A roar of flames and a loud crash issued from the attic.

"Go for it," Drew said.

Slight though I was, it was a very tight squeeze. Wriggling, aided by Drew from above, I made it at last and wrapping my hands and ankles around the water pipe, I went shinning down to the floor. "Did it!"

Drew's face appeared above, a white blur. "Hurry! The smoke's getting through! Find the toolbox!"

I tried the light switch, letting out a sob of relief when the small high-hanging bulb blazed into life. On a shelf amongst the dusters and tins of polish was the toolbox. Inside was a hammer with prongs at one end.

"Hurry!" Drew urged again. He reached down, hand flapping wildly.

Against the wall was the stepladder Josie used for reaching the top shelves. Clattering up it, I handed Drew the tool, and with a few deft strokes, the floorboards were lifted. Seconds later Drew was at my side, wet and smudged with dirt.

"Which bedroom is Mrs. Carew's? She might be in there."

"It's the first one," I said.

We looked but she wasn't there. "Better check the other rooms," Drew said. "It would be quicker if we split up. You do this passage, I'll do the other. Make sure and close the doors or the fire will spread. Hurry!"

All too aware of the terrible danger, we tore off. Flinging open doors, peering into the bedrooms, moving on. As we searched, we shouted.

"Mrs. Carew? Mrs. Ca…rew!"

Our voices fell on neatly kept rooms depressingly void of human life. "Mrs. Carew!" I hollered into the one at the end of the passage. No answer. Ominous crackling sounds came from above. Running back to the top of the stairs, I met Drew, disheveled and out of breath.

"Any luck?" he gasped.

I shook my head, droplets of water flying. "No."

"Downstairs then. Damn Trish! She should be lynched!"

We raced down the wide stairway and made another frenzied search of the ground floor rooms. Drew ventured into the cellar, but there was no sign of Mrs. Carew.

"She's got to be here somewhere!" I said. "Let's look in the stables. Grab the keys. They're by the door."

Outside, a lurid orange glow lit the attic windows. I ran to the barn to release the dogs, who leaped around me joyfully. From the top of the house came an explosion of glass and a gable window blew out, cascading down onto the gravel path in a glistening shower of amber and crimson shards. I stood transfixed, watching in horror as a tongue of scarlet flame licked out, billowing smoke. The dogs all started to bark. From the paddock came a frightened whinny.

"Hope Magpie's all right," Drew muttered, casting an anxious glance in the direction of the trees beyond the high boundary wall. "Wish the phone was on! Damn Trish!"

The looseboxes were all closed up. We ran along the row, looking inside every one. We looked in the tack room and lost valuable seconds locating the key on the bunch for the coach house and padlocked box. No sign of Mrs. Carew anywhere.

"What now?" said Drew.

The dogs, thoroughly upset, were whimpering pitifully. "Jet! Find Jane!" I said. "Find her."

For a moment Jet looked as if he had not understood, then with a woof of comprehension he dropped his nose to the ground and began to sniff. He caught a scent and set off, the other two in his wake.

"Come on," Drew said, heading after them along the grass track that bordered the paddocks. The ponies were all milling around, wild-eyed, uneasy. From beyond the garden wall, Magpie let out a frightened squeal and yanked backwards, scuffling, fighting his tether. In an instant he gained his freedom and went thundering off.

"He'll be OK." Drew panted. "He'll go home! Bet he's broken his reins. Damn!"

The dogs, well into their stride now, charged across the bottom paddock where Lucy and her foal were galloping recklessly up and down. The dogs headed for the open field shelter in the far corner and vanished inside. Gleeful barks followed.

"They've got her." Drew grabbed my hand. "Come on!"

We found Mrs. Carew sitting unceremoniously on a bale of straw, all three dogs licking her face and wagging their tails madly. Her hands and feet were bound with baling twine and she was gagged with the scarf she'd been wearing. Her eyes above the sky-blue silk were blisteringly indignant.

"It's OK, Mrs. Carew," I said, removing the gag while Drew dealt with her bonds. "There. Are you all right?"

"I am. No thanks to Trish!" she snapped, massaging her sore wrists. "Whatever came over the woman? Wait till I get my hands on her! I'll – what now?"

The wail of a distant siren pierced the night. It was coming closer.

"Sounds like the fire department!" Drew said with some relief. "Thank goodness. I'm going to open the gates."

He went sprinting off across the paddock, sending the mare and foal galloping around again in high dudgeon. Mrs. Carew had now risen to her feet and was standing in the open entrance to the shelter, staring in shocked disbelief at her house where flames were now raging from the upper windows.

"What next?" she exclaimed faintly.

Next was Mom, hysterically sobbing my name as she tore toward us over the grass, blue cotton skirt billowing around her racing legs. Here, she pulled up short.

"Mother!" she gasped.

Mrs. Carew's face crumpled. "Oh, Anna Louise!"

140

Chapter Eleven

Gaining a grandmother who also happened to be the daunting owner of Hayes End was hard to take in. For days I walked around in shock, Yet it was the very nicest type of trauma, and the joyful hugging and kissing that went on had to be seen to be believed. Mom told of how, as newlyweds who had eloped, she and Dad had fled to his family in America. Time had gone by, making the rift with home increasingly difficult to breach. She told of how after Dad died, it seemed all the more important to do so, no matter what.

"When the teaching post cropped up at Ravenshill, it seemed destined. Every morning I told myself I'd go and try to make my peace with Mother, only I still kept putting it off. Silly me!" Mom said, shame-faced.

More hugs followed; weepy, forgiving ones. It was as though the lost years were rinsed away and everyone had come up sparkling and ready to get on with life.

It turned out that Bryce had spied the blaze and called the fire department. Then Mom had appeared, thrilled at having pulled off first place at the festival. Her delight was quashed by the shock of seeing the night lit by flames as the minibus approached home. When she realized it was Hayes End ablaze, she made the driver drop her off there. Seeing me had been an even bigger shock.

"Some baby-sitter you turned out to be!" she said wryly to Bryce.

"Sorry." He turned down his mouth, affecting guilt, his eyes twinkling.

We were sitting in the kitchen, drinking coffee out of Mom's best bone china cups, Gran Carew not being the type to drink from a mug.

"Baby indeed!" sniffed my new grandparent. "Shelley's a young woman and a very capable one too. If it hadn't been for her, and Drew of course, things might have been much worse."

The firefighters had done an excellent job at quenching the flames, but the damage to the upper story of the house was extensive. While the insurance claim was being settled and repairs done, Gran Carew and the dogs were staying with us.

Right from when I had turned up at Hayes End seeking a job, Gran had spotted a striking resemblance in me to her long lost daughter. It had not taken much to delve into our background and find out the truth.

I recalled that baffling E-mail from Bryce, and part of the puzzle slid illuminatingly into place. I knew now why Mom had been so reluctant to be seen around the village and at Dalewood. Someone would have been certain to recognize her.

Someone had.

"That Trish!" Mom said, shaking her head in disbelief. "Who would have believed it? Breaking into our cottage as well, just to make sure we were who she thought we were. I suppose Shelley and I do look alike."

"Two peas in a pod," Bryce endorsed with a smile. "Those photo studies that Miles took would have convinced her – he was a promising photographer even when she knew him. Then there's that family shot of the three of you. She'd have recognized all of you from that. Could be that in her confused state she even took Shelley for her old pal Anna Louise. A deranged mind can follow bizarre routes."

Just then Drew appeared at the door. "Come on in," Mom said. "Coffee?"

"Please," Drew said, sliding into a ladder-backed wooden chair next to me and accepting his drink. "I wondered if you'd heard any news of Trish? I know she was picked up wandering demented on the moor. There are all sorts of stories circulating in the village. I don't know what to believe."

"No," Gran said repressively. "Poor unhinged creature. She was such a willing girl and very good with the ponies."

"What will happen to her now?" Mom wondered.

Gran put down her coffee. "I won't be pressing charges, if that's what you mean. Trish needs professional treatment and that's what she'll get. None of us has come to any harm. The fire was an accident – well, candles are always risky. When the repairs are being done, I shall have the attic properly wired for electricity."

"There's Shelley," Mom said, indignant. "That bump on the head could have been serious."

Mom had insisted on having me checked out at the hospital. They had diagnosed slight concussion and kept me in overnight for observation. All my symptoms had faded and next morning I came happily home.

"But it wasn't, was it?" Gran said. "On the whole events have turned out far better than they might have for us all. And," she said, sliding a look at Mom, "who knows how long it might have taken the two of us to come around and start talking to each other if the whole thing hadn't happened. In a way, I suppose we owe the poor girl a debt of gratitude."

"True," Bryce said. He sat back in his chair, his arms folded across his chest. "You got the trophy back too. Lucky it didn't perish in the fire."

It was in safe hands, a solid gold figurine, not large, the face and figure bearing a startling resemblance to the one I had glimpsed at the cave. Local Heritage suspected the effigy stemmed from an age almost as old as time itself.

"Did you find out what else Trish was doing up in the attic?" said Drew.

"Yes," said Gran. "Apparently she was looking for some old stud papers I'd put away up there. Like me, Trish recognized Hayes End breeding in Silver Rocket. Maybe she had ideas about breeding something like him herself. Whatever, while she was on the premises she seized the opportunity to look up the pedigrees."

We all stared at her. "Hayes End breeding?" I echoed, dumbfounded.

Gran then told us of the mare and foal that Matthew Oaks had spoken of, and how they had escaped the yard without a trace. It was clear now who that mare had been.

"It was Trustful, wasn't it?" I said. "Was that why her details weren't with the others in the study?"

"That's right." Gran said with a sigh. "It happened

144

during that bad patch in our lives. Anna Louise was gone, her father wasn't in very good health. Losing Trustful seemed like the very last straw. This was before the days of security systems and organized round-ups, remember. Any pony that got loose on the moor stood a dim chance of being found. I decided to draw a line under the whole sorry business and removed the papers to the attic with the other defunct stuff. We'd registered the foal with the name Torquil. I suspect that Rocket descends from him."

"I really loved Trustful." Mom's eyes were misty. "I named her after an earlier Trustful, remember? I wasn't very old. I'd underlined the name on the old pedigree certificate in red ink because I liked it so much. I got into big trouble for scribbling on important documents! She… she wouldn't still be out there, would she?"

"I doubt it," Gran said gently. "Trustful would have been a very old lady by now. But her son Torquil could be still around. He might even be the stallion that's running with the current herd. Trustful's was my best line. I shall look into the matter." Her eyes gleamed.

"But why did you buy Rocket?" Drew asked in some confusion. "He wouldn't have been any use to the yard. It wasn't as if he was a mare that could have been bred from. And he's a gelding, after all."

Gran shook her head. "No. I bought Rocket for Shelley – he was to be a kind of peace offering. When I found out who she was, I didn't know how to broach the subject. My daughter might not have wanted to make peace after all those lost and wasted years. And who could blame her? This seemed like a good way of going about a new start. Only it all went wrong."

I colored up. "Me and my temper! Oh, I *wish* we knew where Rocket is. I've looked everywhere. He's just vanished."

"He could have been rounded up," Drew commented. "The auction people have been out there since first light."

"Oh?" I stared at him. "So when's the auction?"

"Tomorrow," Drew said. "I thought you knew. Starts at nine sharp."

Everyone started to talk at once. Bryce sent me a wink of encouragement. "We'll be there," he said.

***

The auction ground heaved with horses, ponies, and people milling about damply in the soaking upland drizzle. Dogs ran barking underfoot and the reek of horse and trampled dung was ripe on the air. Bryce, Drew, Mom, and I had arrived early to scan the pens before the bidding started. Gran had opted not to come, having things to do at Hayes End. Until the house was habitable again, Matthew and Josie Oaks were living on site in a mobile home, in order to keep an eye on the yard.

"In any case, you'll manage better without me," Gran had said. "Good luck."

Up and down the rows of pens we wove, inspecting every animal. Grays of all types were on show; dappled-gray, light gray, moon-colored, but none of them was Silver Rocket. In a far pen, a dark steel-gray head sent me pushing hopefully through the crowd for a closer look, but it turned out to be a two-year-old filly and not Rocket at all. With dragging steps I went to the others.

"It's no good," I said. "We'll never find him amongst all these. I never expected so many."

"It always was a big event," said Mom doubtfully. "Let's go and eat. Then we can decide what do to next."

In the auction-ground snack bar, farmers and dealers were sitting at the tables arguing prices, while waitresses tore up and down with loaded carts of food and drink. Bryce ordered coffee for Mom and himself, sodas for me and Drew, and baguettes, since none of us had eaten much breakfast. We had just begun eating, when the close circuit television screen above the self-service area flashed into life. Simultaneously the speaker system, which was piped all over the auction ground, emitted an ear-splitting screech and the voice of the auctioneer boomed out, announcing the commencement of the sale.

"And now ladies and gentlemen let's make a start with the unwarranted section with lot number one."

With interest we watched as the number appeared on the screen. Once the bidding was in progress, the price the animal on auction was currently making showed up as well. Bidding was brisk and the animal, a yearling colt, was knocked down for a princely four hundred pounds. Lot number two was brought in and the auction-eer launched eagerly into his spiel.

"And what have we here, everyone? A truly handsome steel-gray gelding." I sat up, electrified. "Five years old, believed broken, good to handle –"

"That's him!" I squeaked, slamming my drink down on the table. "Come on!"

Cups were hastily returned to saucers, slopping rivulets of coffee over the varnished wooden tabletop. Chairs scraped on the hard tiles of the floor and we all

jumped to our feet, making a rush for the exit. The main hall was at the farthest end of the auction-ground. Ducking our heads against the drizzle, we ran for it.

Drew and I got there first. Panting, we elbowed through the crush of speculators around the entrance and reached the huge vaulted amphitheater, where the warm smell of horse, rain-wet clothes, and the takeaway burgers sold at a stand at the back of the building enfolded us.

"There's a space," Drew said, indicating a standing place by the front rails that offered a good view. Standing at the lectern, the auctioneer was still rattling off the particulars, stressing the animal's good points and cleverly glossing over his lack of height, which would effectively put him out of most areas of competition work. In the pit, a boy in frayed jeans and a scruffy sweatshirt was leading Silver Rocket around on a rope halter.

"Want me to bid for you?" Drew asked.

"Oh, would you?" I said gratefully. "I've never been to an auction before. I wouldn't know where to start."

"What's your limit?"

"Five hundred and that's it."

Panic choked my voice. I glanced around the hall at the sea of faces. Most were here with the object of purchasing the animal of their dreams. Surely I wasn't going to lose Rocket now?

The auctioneer cleared his throat noisily. "Right, ladies and gentleman, you've seen the goods. Who'll start me off at six hundred?"

"Oh no!" I squeaked, unable to believe what I had heard.

"It's OK," Drew said hastily. "They always do that to start off. He'll drop down, you'll see."

Sure enough, the next sum was a more reasonable two

hundred. A man in a brown quilted jacket near the exit nodded his head.

"Thank you, sir. Two-twenty-five? Anyone for two-twenty-five?"

The auctioneer's gimlet eyes swept the hall, taking in the tiered rows of seating, the standing area on the balcony, and the people thronged near the entrance and the exit. At my side, Drew stood alert but puzzlingly silent. An oldish man in a combat coat near us made a show of rubbing his nose. The auctioneer recognized the action of a second player and the bidding commenced, going up rapidly.

"Drew," I said in an agony of suspense. "Make a bid."

"Quiet. It'll only push up the price. Wait till one of them drops out."

It happened at three hundred and fifty. The man near us shook his head and thrust his fists firmly into his coat pockets.

"Any other bidders?" the auctioneer asked, raking the hall with another keen glance.

This time, Drew raised his hand.

"Young gentleman at the front rails. Thank you, sir." Confidently the auctioneer pitched again into the running, his head darting from us to the man at the entrance. "Three-sixty? Three-sixty-five? Three-seventy?" The gavel waved to and fro. "Four hundred?

Behind us there was a stir and Mom and Bryce arrived, very out of breath.

"We got held up," Mom said in my ear. "They were running some ponies across the track. What are we at? Four hundred? Heavens – I don't think I can stand the strain!"

"Four hundred and twenty-five. Four-thirty." On the big wide electronic display board above the rostrum, the figures went whizzing up. "Four hundred and eighty. Four hundred and eighty-five."

"Drew," I choked. "It's going to go over. I won't have enough."

The auctioneer paused. "Five hundred clear?"

He looked across at Drew, and with commendable calm, Drew raised his hand.

Smirking, the auctioneer took the plunge and drastically upped his price. "Five hundred and fifty? Come on now. Who'll give me five-fifty for this fine all-purpose gelding, a bargain at the price?"

The other man nodded his head again.

My heart dropped. The auctioneer glanced encouragingly at us. The man in the jacket began to smirk.

"I haven't got it," I said in a small voice.

Again the auctioneer looked to Drew.

"Go for it!" said Bryce suddenly from behind. Drew flung up his hand and off we went again. At five hundred and seventy the man in the brown jacket shook his head.

"Any more bidders?"

Forcefully the auctioneer tried for more, his wooden gavel raised, his eyes searching every corner of the hall in the hope of a late bidder. The auditorium had gone silent. I could hear my heart thumping, my breath coming in short gasps. "Going once. Going a second time. I can't linger... Sold – to the young lady and gentleman at the front rails." The gavel hit the lectern with a thwack.

Silver Rocket was mine!

***

"Have you had the results of the DNA test yet?" Drew asked, giving Magpie a nudge to keep up with Rocket who jogged spiritedly along. We were hacking out before school. Around us, the moor lay under the hazy sunrise of a perfect September day.

"Yes," I said eagerly. "It came in yesterday's post. It's positive. Rocket's by the moor stallion all right, out of a moorland mare."

"Pure bred then – wow!" Drew grinned at me with delight. "What about the stallion?" The splodgy black horse, rough-coated and wily after years on the moor, had been caught and brought to Hayes End for the testing. "Is it Torquil?"

"Yes again. Gran's having him freeze-branded, then she's turning him back out again with the herd. She says it would be cruel to keep him in a paddock after living wild all this time. She's got plans to use him on a couple of mares next spring."

"Great. Well. You'll be eligible for the registered classes now. Next year, how about entering Rocket for Ravenshill Show?"

"It's a thought." Fondly I stroked Rocket's arching gray neck. "I love him to bits. If Rocket never wins a single rosette he'll still be the best ever."

"I know exactly what you mean. I feel the same way about Magpie. He's nothing much to look at, won't jump, is useless at dressage, but there'll never be another like him for me. All the same, you've got a good prospect in Rocket. It'll be interesting to see how he goes." Drew paused. "Shelley. There's something I want to ask you."

"Yes?"

"There's this gig at the youth club in town. It's a jazz group playing. I've got tickets. Would you like to come?"

Blushing, I smiled at him. "Love to."

"I sometimes play there myself. The resident group are looking for a flautist and I mentioned your name. They're a great bunch. You interested?"

"I might be," I said.

I'd need something new to wear, I thought happily. I wondered if Mom would let me borrow her jet beads. Mom, who like me, had experienced the ancient power of Hob Tor. A good power. Quietly she had told me how, when the vet had given up all hope for her lame pony, she had appealed to the horse witch by carving Trustful's image in the cave – and the final piece of the puzzle had slipped satisfyingly into place.

Tonight Mom and Bryce were taking Gran and me out for dinner. Bryce would be going home the next day, but not for long I suspected. They might have a special announcement to make, they said. I hoped I knew what it was. No one would ever replace Dad, but I couldn't imagine a nicer stepfather than Bryce, and I know Dad would have been pleased for all of us too.

Just then, the horses' ears shot forward and their heads came up. Over the hillocks a line of ponies appeared. We reined in, listening to that heart-stopping pulse of hooves growing ever louder as the racing herd fanned out and came galloping toward us over the springy upland turf. They streamed past in a mass of straining muscle and steaming, hard-packed flesh, filling me with joy as they had that very first time I had seen them, when horse was just a word in a book.

"Good, eh?" Drew said softly.

"Very good," I replied.

And with the sound of hoofbeats still trembling in our ears, we gathered up our reins and rode together for home.